Other Yearling Books you will enjoy:

FOOTSTEPS ON THE STAIRS, *C. S. Adler*
THE HAUNTING OF CASSIE PALMER, *Vivien Alcock*
THE SUMMER BIRDS, *Penelope Farmer*
THE GRIFFIN LEGACY, *Jan O'Donnel Klaveness*
THE THING AT THE FOOT OF THE BED, *Maria Leach*
THE GHOSTS OF COUGAR ISLAND, *Peggy Parish*
PIRATE ISLAND ADVENTURE, *Peggy Parish*
KEY TO THE TREASURE, *Peggy Parish*
HERMIT DAN, *Peggy Parish*
HAUNTED HOUSE, *Peggy Parish*

MOSTLY GHOSTS

The
Haunting
of
Hillcrest

by Mary Anderson

A YEARLING BOOK

Published by
Dell Publishing Co., Inc.
1 Dag Hammarskjold Plaza
New York, New York 10017

Yearling ® TM 913705, Dell Publishing Co., Inc.

ISBN: 0-440-43372-X

Printed in the United States of America

September 1987

10 9 8 7 6 5 4 3 2 1

CW

The
Haunting
of
Hillcrest

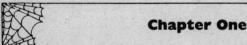

AMY WAS WORRIED. SHE'D GOTTEN ONE OF HER STRANGE FEELINGS again, which meant something bad was going to happen. She didn't know what it would be, but it was going to happen *soon*.

As usual she was tempted to tell her twin brother, Jamie, about it—but as usual she didn't.

I've kept this secret from him all my life, she told herself, *so why tell him now? No one's going to call* me *a freak. And no one's going to say I'm weird, just because I see and know things no one else does.*

As Jamie walked into the room his sister finished her internal discussion by resolving continued silence. "What's with you?" he asked. "Why are you staring like a dead fish?"

"None of your business," she said coolly as she watched

1

her brother put the finishing touches on his costume for the school play. He was adjusting the derby hat, which was definitely several sizes too large, while glancing at himself questioningly in the mirror. "If you must know," she added, trying to take her mind off her upsetting premonition, "I was thinking how silly you look in that outfit."

Jamie frowned. He already had major misgivings (not to mention a major case of stage fright) about playing the part of Alexander Cartwright, the founder of their school. Did twelve-year-olds get heart attacks? he wondered. "It *does* look silly," he said aloud. "I *told* Miss Apthorp, but she insists on authenticity."

The twins realized that when Miss Apthorp, their headmistress, insisted on something, she got it. Once she had decided to put on a dramatization of the life of Alexander Cartwright in celebration of the fiftieth anniversary of the school, that was that! Their father often said Miss Apthorp ran things "with an iron hand." When the children were younger, they took that statement literally. Miss Apthorp had a habit of holding her hands behind her back, so naturally they had assumed she was hiding that strange iron robot hand. Of course, they now knew it meant Miss Apthorp was a persistent woman with very definite standards—standards Jamie feared he wouldn't measure up to in his starring role as Alexander Cartwright.

Jamie adjusted the hat for the tenth time. "Old Appy should've picked someone with *acting talent*," he grumbled.

Amy agreed. "Yeah, like Colin Williamson. But he's a

rotten student, and Miss A. insisted the person with the best marks get the part."

"But I'm a seventh-grader. Why didn't she pick an *eighth*-grade student?"

"*No* student has better marks than yours, Jamie."

"That's true, but it's not fair. I shouldn't have to suffer just because I'm brilliant!"

Mrs. Ferguson entered the living room to admire her son's costume. "What's this I hear about suffering?" she asked. "Jamie, you look splendid. Except for that hat," she added. "Don't smash it down over your ears like that; the audience will want to see your face."

"That's right." Amy giggled. "If they're looking at his face, they might not notice that his knees are knocking."

"Don't tease your brother," Mr. Ferguson said between gulps of his morning coffee. "I think he already has stage fright."

For a moment Amy felt like admitting *she* was frightened too. She was teasing her brother to relieve her own fear—a fear that something terrible would happen during the play. But admitting that would also be admitting she'd often had such premonitions before—and that when she did, the terrible things she feared *always* came true. She remembered the time Sarah Richardson had fallen down the stairs at school. In her mind Amy had seen it happen hours earlier. And once, Mom had left chicken frying on the stove. Even though Amy was in school at the time, she'd seen their kitchen going up in flames. Luckily the fire department had put out the blaze in time. But Amy's latest vision was different. This time she

3

couldn't actually see the details of the awful thing that would soon happen. Perhaps that meant it wouldn't happen after all.

"Well, why are we all standing around?" asked Mr. Ferguson. "Wasn't there some purpose to my canceling all my morning classes? Don't tell me my college history majors will be starving for knowledge for no good reason."

"Oh, there's a reason," Jamie groaned. "It's to see me make a fool of myself in public."

"Fine talk," said Mrs. Ferguson. "You'll be great. And you'll also be *on time,* so let's get moving."

As they hurried toward the door Jamie glanced at himself once more in the entrance hall mirror, hoping to give himself confidence. He didn't. "A twelve-year-old dressed in a three-piece suit definitely looks like an *idiot*. And when I open my mouth, I'm sure I'll sound like one too!"

Chapter Two

IT WAS DEFINITELY A SPECIAL DAY AT HILLCREST ACADEMY: ALL morning classes had been canceled, which no doubt would account for the unusually large number of smiling faces entering the building. The biggest smile of all was on the face of Jemima Apthorp as she stood outside the school's wood-paneled doors greeting the children as they entered. Personally greeting each student each morning was something Miss Apthorp considered both a pleasure and a responsibility. Religiously she would be there in the entrance hall—a large, plump sentinel officiating at the opening of another "invigorating educational day."

The children loved to make comments about that. "Has she grown roots, or what?" David Toshito always asked. "Can't she ever oversleep?" Sandra Bentley would complain. Rain or shine, Miss Apthorp was there, seemingly more solid and durable than the heavy oak paneling of the doors behind her. This was *her* school and she took a proprietary interest in everything that happened inside its walls, just as her mother, Amanda Apthorp, had done before her. Not one pencil dropped without Miss A. knowing all about it!

"Hurry along, children," she said. "Everyone please go to the auditorium. I want everything to run on schedule this morning. It's going to be a wonderfully special day!"

Jamie had big misgivings about that. He had gone over his lines a thousand times in his head, and he had them letter-perfect, but he still hated the idea of being the center of attention onstage. Jamie could easiy solve an intricate puzzle, reason out a math equation, or devise a complicated program for the school computer, but he couldn't act, and he knew it. He was afraid that by twelve o'clock, when the play was over, everyone else would know it too!

"All my actors please proceed backstage for a final briefing," Miss Apthorp announced. "All relatives and parents of performers please take your seats of honor in the first five rows."

"I guess that's us," said Mr. Ferguson. "We'll be right up front watching you, Son."

"I know that, Dad; that's the problem."

"You'll be fine," Jamie's mother told him reassuringly. "Just think positively."

"I can't think at all. I'm sure I'll do something stupid."

"That's just stage fright; it'll go away," Amy said unconvincingly.

6

"Hold it," said Jamie, grabbing his sister's hand. "Come backstage with me for a minute, okay?"

"Sure. But why?"

"Do I have to spell it out for you? I'm *nervous*."

It was a rare occasion when Jamie asked his sister for moral support, so she knew he wasn't kidding. Amy wanted to tell him to relax, but her awful premonition wouldn't let her. She, too, wished twelve o'clock would come quickly so the whole ordeal would be over.

Downstairs in the auditorium all the other actors had assembled backstage, awaiting Miss Apthorp's inspection. In military fashion the headmistress surveyed their costumes, making last-minute adjustments. She seemed surprised when she approached Heidi Wentworth, who was portraying Miss Apthorp's mother, the first headmistress.

"What are those *bulges* under your dress, dear?"

"Padding," Heidi explained proudly. "I've stuffed it full of towels to make me look fatter. And I put lots of eyebrow pencil lines on my face to age me. I thought it would make me *look* the part."

Miss Apthorp cleared her throat. "Yes—well—that's very effective. But one must *feel* the part as well. Just think strength and determination; that was the keynote of my mother's personality."

"Yes, ma'am."

Miss Apthorp glanced at Jamie. "Why on earth is that hat seated on your head in such a strange manner?"

"It doesn't fit," he said solemnly.

"Well, stuff it!"

7

The entire cast began to giggle.

"This isn't a moment for levity," she scolded. "Here, I've just the thing." Removing a scarf from around her neck, Miss Apthorp wedged it along the rim of the bowler hat and placed it back on Jamie's head. "There, now you look like a true man of distinction."

As Amy stood beside the stage, a strange wave of anxiety passed through her body. She wanted to shout out to her brother that something terrible was soon to happen. To *him*. But what *was* it?

"Amy, why are you standing there?" asked Miss Apthorp. "Take your seat in the audience. The curtain's going up shortly."

"Yes, but . . ."

"Do you want to wish your brother good luck first? Actually I think 'break a leg' is the appropriate expression. Well, go ahead, child, but hurry."

Jamie was still fiddling with his wretched hat, only now he was complaining because he couldn't hear with the scarf wedged inside of it.

"That's it," said Amy in sudden realization. "It has something to do with that *hat*!"

"What does?" Jamie asked. "What do you mean?"

No matter how hard Amy tried, the picture wouldn't become any clearer in her mind. "Oh, nothing. Just be careful. Promise me you'll be careful, all right?"

"If you're trying to relieve my fears, you're doing a crummy job of it, Amy."

"I'm sorry. It's just that sometimes I . . ." She hesitated.

"Sometimes you what?"

"Think a person should be careful—that's all."

"Yeah, well, sometimes I think a person shouldn't get straight A's, so he won't be forced into stardom. I'll see you after the show—if I'm still *alive*, that is."

Jamie's last words rang through his sister's ears with prophetic implications. "Don't say that," she said emphatically. "You won't *die*."

"Of course I won't, you nut. Hey, I think you're more nervous than *I* am."

It was true. Amy was now convinced that whatever danger was present onstage, it involved her brother—and it would happen shortly.

She could feel herself shaking as she took her seat in the audience. How could she stop something when she didn't know what it was? And why should that silly hat have anything to do with it? Every other time she'd had a vision of some disaster, she could see it clearly—but not this time. Did that mean it was something that *might* happen? If so, what could she do to prevent it?

Once the audience had settled down, Miss Apthorp took center stage. "Greetings, faculty of Hillcrest, parents, and students. And welcome to staff members of the *Monroe Gazette* who will be covering this event for our local paper. As you all know, this is our school's fiftieth anniversary. Our dear benefactor, Alexander Cartwright, deeded this land and property to us years ago. Today's dramatization will commemorate that event. Let me add, I've arranged a special luncheon for everyone after the final curtain. So now let's sit back and share this happy moment together."

9

The curtains parted, the lights went up, and the play began. The first act depicted Alexander Cartwright's travels throughout the world and the many interesting and famous people he had met. The second act explained how he had built a fine mansion in Monroe County, filling it with artifacts, rare books, and collectibles from around the globe. The third act described how he had deeded the entire property to the town, to be turned into an educational academy with Miss Apthorp's mother as its first headmistress.

By some miracle Jamie managed to survive the first two acts without messing up his lines; but it wasn't easy, because the padding in his hat made it difficult for him to hear his cues. Slowly, as the play progressed, Jamie gained confidence. (At least nobody had begun laughing out loud as yet!)

Jamie prepared himself for the final big scene in the last act when he would hand over the ownership deed to Amanda Apthorp. He glanced at Heidi Wentworth. She looked ridiculous with all those towels stuffed inside her dress. For one reckless moment Jamie felt like pulling them out of her blouse and waving them in the air, but he restrained himself. Only one more scene to go and the whole horrible ordeal would be over. Then he could retire for life and never set foot on a stage again!

As Jamie glanced out at the darkened figures in the audience, his eyes made contact with Amy, who sat in the first row. What was that strange expression on her face? he wondered. Her eyes seemed to be burning into his, as if she were trying to *tell* him something. Distracted, Jamie nearly forgot his lines, but Heidi covered up by grabbing the deed to Hillcrest from his hands.

"Thank you so much, Mr. Cartwright," she said. "Now this town will have a wonderful school and we will teach here forever. I think I'll call it Hillcrest Academy. Your gift will light our children's way to knowledge."

As Heidi smiled toward the audience, a strange, unsettling noise came suddenly from above. All the cast members looked up to see what had caused it—all but Jamie. With the padding inside his hat, he was unable to hear the noise.

In that instant Amy's prophetic vision came into focus: She could see her brother's body lying crumpled on the stage, covered with shards of shattered glass. Now she stood up and shouted, "Move, Jamie—*quickly*!" just seconds before one of the stage lights came shattering to the ground.

Jamie heard her warning just in time. Within moments the light suspended from the wires overhead fell to the ground in the exact spot where Jamie had been standing. It had just missed him by inches.

A gasp rose up from the entire audience, and Miss Apthorp rushed onto the stage. Once she was assured no one had been hurt, she made an announcement. "I'm sincerely sorry for the overly dramatic ending to our play. But all the children are safe and unharmed, and I'm sure we all agree they gave a splendid performance."

The audience, relieved the near disaster was over, broke out in loud applauding.

"What a close call," Mrs. Ferguson said with a sigh.

"Amy, if you hadn't seen that light begin to fall, Jamie would have been seriously hurt."

"How did you notice it so quickly?" asked her father. "It was all over before I ever knew what had happened."

Amy didn't dare tell them the truth. "I don't know; I guess I have good eyesight."

"And quick reasoning," he added. "If you hadn't shouted like that— Well, thank God you did!"

Amy thanked God too. Whatever her strange gift was, it had saved Jamie from being hurt.

The cast members were now greeting their parents in the audience. Jamie himself pretended to take the whole thing lightly. "I certainly started my acting career with a *bang*, didn't I?"

"Don't joke about it, Son. You were almost in a nasty accident."

"I can't understand how it happened," said Mrs. Ferguson. "Miss Apthorp has always been so careful about maintaining stage equipment."

"And everything else," her husband agreed. "She runs this place like a general. Well, it just goes to prove that accidents can happen *anywhere*."

Amy was silent. Her dreadful premonition had passed, but she still felt uneasy. Something inside was telling her it hadn't been an *accident*!

When the children and guests arrived in the lunchroom of Hillcrest Academy, they saw that it had been transformed. Miss Apthorp had hired a special catering service for the occasion. Instead of the usual bare metal

12

tables and plastic trays, there were fancy linens, china plates, fresh flowers, and streams of white balloons.

It truly looked like a banquet—with not one peanut butter sandwich or squashed milk carton as far as the eye could see. In their place were tiny open-faced sandwiches, dishes of fresh fruit salad, a giant crystal punch bowl, and a huge assortment of chips and dips. The food was served by waiters in starched white shirts and black silk ties. Some of the smaller children actually missed their traditional peanut butter, but everyone else seemed to prefer the fancy ham, salmon, and roast beef sandwiches decorated with raw vegetables shaped like flowers.

Miss Apthorp sat proudly at the center table, with cast members, their parents, and the photographer and reporter from the *Monroe Gazette*. Halfway through the luncheon she began referring to her "special surprise dessert" hidden in the kitchen.

Amy excused herself to go to the bathroom.

"Hurry back," whispered Jamie. "Old Appy is making such a deal about this dessert, you'd better not miss it."

Once the main course was finished, the children became fidgety. Miss Apthorp felt she'd waited long enough to make her special presentation. Clinking a glass with her fork, she stood up. "Now, for the pièce de résistance. For you younger children not yet schooled in French, that means the main dish—translated literally, of course. Actually, I'm referring to our dessert."

Two waiters wheeled in a fancy food cart with a giant bakery box resting on top.

"Young men, please lift the cake so all my guests can see the decoration."

As the waiters slowly lifted the cake everyone stared at it. Then gasps of shock and surprise echoed around the room. Etched across the icing in globs of black frosting was a huge skull and crossbones!

No one knew what to make of it. Judging from Miss Apthorp's face, it didn't seem to be a joke.

Henry Reeves, a first-grader, yelled out: "I don't wanna eat poison cake, Miss Apthorp. My mom says a skeleton sign means poison and to stay away."

Miss Apthorp stopped smiling and stared at him. "A *skeleton*? No, dear, this is a replica of Hillcrest." She turned to glance at the cake herself and nearly fell over in surprise. "What on earth is *that*? I specifically ordered a cake with a miniature of our school outlined in blue frosting. What is that gruesome thing doing there instead?"

The waiters looked confused. "I don't know, ma'am," one of them said. "It wasn't there when the cake left the catering shop."

"Don't be ridiculous," she said sharply. "Skulls don't just appear on top of cakes. *Someone* must have put it there."

"I don't know, ma'am," the waiter repeated blankly.

Miss Apthorp seemed both concerned and upset. Realizing her reaction might be frightening the younger children, she tried now to treat the incident as just a silly mistake. "Well, perhaps we mistakenly received a cake meant for *pirates*, isn't that right, children?"

At the mention of the word *pirates* several students

14

started laughing. "Let's have some pirate cake," shouted the first-graders, who finally began to feel that it was a real party.

"Old Appy wiggled out of that one neatly," Jamie noted. "All things considered, this has been an extremely peculiar morning."

Amy nodded but said nothing. She sensed that whatever weird things were going on at Hillcrest, they had only just begun!

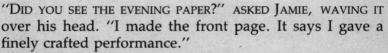

Chapter Three

"Did you see the evening paper?" asked Jamie, waving it over his head. "I made the front page. It says I gave a finely crafted performance."

"Naturally," said his mother, who was setting the table. "Everything went really well."

"Not according to this headline," he said, reading it aloud: " 'near fatal accident at hillcrest.' "

"Let's see that," said his father. Reading through the article, he was obviously displeased. "Miss Apthorp will be furious about this bad publicity. That reporter over-dramatized the broken stage light and the vandalized cake. He speculates that it might have some sinister implications."

"Well, Dad, I guess he had to do something dramatic to get his byline on the front page. But the important thing is he thought I was good, right?"

16

Mrs. Ferguson glanced through the article. "Oh, dear, there's even a picture of that dreadful cake."

"It wasn't dreadful," Jamie protested. "Bizarre and peculiar maybe, but still delicious, so what's it matter?"

Amy didn't agree. "If Appy is going to be furious, it matters. She's been acting odd since school began, and now she's going to be even flakier."

Jamie was annoyed that his successful performance had somehow gotten overshadowed in the conversation. "Don't *I* get any attention around here? Who cares if Miss A. gets mad or not?"

"*We* do," said Amy.

There was no denying it: Miss Apthorp's state of mind was always an important factor at Hillcrest. The twins' parents had also attended the school, so they knew exactly what Amy meant.

"You're right," Mr. Ferguson said. "I can remember Miss Apthorp's wrath vividly. Once when I was ten, I was summoned to her office because I'd placed an olfactory experiment in the art supply closet."

"A *what*?" asked Amy.

"Dad means a stink bomb," Jamie explained.

"Yes. Well, semantics aside," Mr. Ferguson continued, "I didn't think I'd come out of her office alive. But Miss A. was actually quite forgiving."

"I once had a run-in with her too," Mrs. Ferguson confessed. "But I always liked her," she quickly added. "She may have been harsh at times, but she was never unfair. So if she's being unpleasant lately, there must be a good reason."

17

"Well, kids at school don't think so," Amy complained. "Things have been rotten all month. In fact, lots of students have threatened to play practical jokes on her."

"Really?" her father said. "Perhaps someone already has. That cake certainly turned Miss Apthorp's big celebration into something of a joke."

As the Fergusons sat down to dinner, the topic of conversation changed. Mrs. Ferguson was having her own problems with quite a different commemorative celebration. As chairman of the fund-raising committee for the Monroe Historical Society, she was responsible for organizing the year's special event. Mrs. Ferguson's ancestors were among the most renowned in Monroe County. Her family tree included judges, politicians, and generals, clear back to the American Revolution.

"I thought we might have an auction this year," she said. "There may be some good items hidden in Papa Tredwell's trunks up in the attic. I've been meaning to go through his things all year, but I haven't gotten to it yet."

"That junk?" asked Amy. "I thought Grandpa just collected old books and diaries."

"Yes, but some of them are very valuable," her mother explained. "Historically speaking, that is. What do you think, Richard? Is an auction a good idea?"

Her husband frowned. "Didn't someone try that two years ago? All anyone donated was broken lamps, cuckoo clocks, and horrible wedding gifts they'd kept hidden in their closets for years."

"I guess you're right," she said, "but I'll have to come up with *something*."

"Well, don't put on a *play*," Jamie cautioned. "I've discovered acting can be hazardous to your health!"

The next day things were back to normal at Hillcrest Academy, except that Miss Apthorp wasn't at the entrance to greet students upon their arrival. For the first time that the twins could remember, the large oak-paneled doors stood unattended.

The absence of Miss A.'s figure in the doorway seemed strangely ominous to Amy. Where could she be? she wondered.

Freddie, the new custodian, was walking through the entrance lobby, frowning. Freddie was *always* either frowning or complaining about the huge amount of work required of him. Children were constantly spilling things on the carpeted marble stairs that led to the classrooms or leaving smudge marks on the oak banisters or scuffing up the parquet floors. Freddie seemed to drag his mops, pails, and dust cloths around as if they were the chains that Marley's ghost was forced to carry through eternity. "I'm not a young man any longer," he kept reminding everyone. "Don't be so careless." Finding a wad of gum stuck to the underside of the banister, he began scraping it off with a palette knife. "Kids don't belong in a fine place like this," he grumbled.

"Where's Miss Apthorp this morning?" Amy asked.

"Minding her own business, I shouldn't wonder," he snapped.

"Who cares where she is?" said Jamie, hurrying up the stairs. "C'mon, we'll be late for English."

Amy wasn't certain why Miss Apthorp's absence concerned her, but it did. She felt it meant something sinister. Then when she noticed a suspicious-looking man speaking with Miss A. outside her office, she was sure of it.

"Who's that?" she asked. "I've never seen *him* around school before. He looks sneaky."

Jamie agreed. The stranger definitely looked suspicious, huddling in the doorway afraid of being seen, and whispering so he wouldn't be heard. "Maybe he's Miss A.'s boyfriend," he joked. "At her age I guess she can't be too choosy. Are you coming to English or not? Mrs. Abernathy is returning our assignments this morning and I want to see my mark."

Amy was in no hurry. She knew she'd receive her usual C while Jamie would get his boringly usual A. Besides, whatever the stranger in the doorway had said, it had definitely upset Miss Apthorp.

As Amy reached the landing she tried to overhear the end of their conversation.

"You've been warned," the man said solemnly. "What happens now is up to you." Pulling the collar of his jacket up to his face, he hurried down the stairs, nearly knocking Amy over.

Obviously upset, Miss Apthorp blew her nose and tried to compose herself. Then she noticed Amy staring at her. "Don't dawdle on the stairs, Amy Ferguson. Get to your classroom at once!"

*　　*　　*

That afternoon the entire school was called to a special assembly. The lingering excitement of the previous day's festivities disappeared when Miss Apthorp made her unexpected announcement.

"I'm understandably upset by the vandalism of our cake yesterday. Until the culprit comes forward, all students must suffer the consequence. As of now, all recreation periods are discontinued, and no student will be allowed outside the main building at any time during the school day."

The students were amazed at the overreaction to what had obviously been a stupid practical joke. Even the teachers seemed surprised.

"No baseball practice?" asked Bud Ridgely, the physical education teacher.

"Absolutely not."

"What about my gardening class?" asked Brenda Folger, the botany instructor.

"Canceled until further notice," Miss Apthorp declared.

"This doesn't make sense," mumbled Jamie. "Why is Appy making such a fuss about that stupid cake?"

Amy agreed it was odd, and quite unlike Miss A. Mom was right: In the past Miss A. had always been stern but fair.

"Well," Jamie continued, "whoever messed it up had better confess real fast."

"It won't happen," said Amy.

"How do you know?" he asked suspiciously.

"I can't tell you; I just know."

21

                            *   *   *

That evening after the twins had finished their home-
work, Jamie went into his sister's room. "Okay," he said,
"come clean."

"About what?" asked Amy.

"Look, I'm your brother, so I won't turn you in, but I
won't miss baseball practice either. Why not throw yourself at old Appy's feet and admit you screwed up her
cake?"

"*Me?* Are you crazy? What makes you think I did
it?"

Jamie was proud of his ability to reason out a situation
logically, so he explained: "Yesterday you were a nervous
wreck, even more nervous than me, so there must've
been some reason for it. Then you excused yourself from
the lunch table just before the cake got wheeled out—you
had just enough time to change the frosting on it. You
also said you *knew* the culprit wouldn't come forward,
which you couldn't know unless you were the culprit. So
you see, simple deductive reasoning tells me *you* did the
dirty deed."

"But I. . . ."

"Hey, it's okay. I said I wouldn't tell, and I won't.
Maybe if you slip a note under Appy's door, she'll accept
your confession without blabbing your name to the whole
school. I'll even help you spell the word *despicable*."

"Very funny, brother dear, but you're out of luck. I
never touched that cake."

"Oh yeah? Well, confession is good for the soul, Amy.

I'm not going to miss baseball practice forever, so think it over!"

When Jamie left the room, Amy did think it over.

Something inside was telling her that something truly *terrible* was happening at school!

Chapter Four

WHEN MISS APTHORP GAVE AN ORDER, SHE MEANT IT!

The next day at Hillcrest there were absolutely no outdoor activities. During classes the younger children looked
out at the play yard, their eyes filled with longing; the
older students, too, stole looks at the sports field and the
garden.

Overnight Hillcrest Academy had become a prison.

In the corridor several of the students were blaming
one another for the problem (just as Jamie had accused
his sister). But no one came forward to admit he'd vandalized the cake.

After Jamie had had some time to think about it, he
soon realized Amy couldn't be the culprit. Sure, she
could be sneaky at times (*very* sneaky), but she would
never do a lousy thing like that! Still, she was defi-

24

nitely hiding something. Shielding the guilty party, maybe?

During math class Jamie finished his work in half the allotted time (as usual), then tried reasoning through the puzzle again. Amy definitely knew something, but he would never be able to get it out of her. All their lives Amy had been secretive, never sharing her personal thoughts or feelings. Sometimes Jamie would watch her stare out into the distance, as if she knew and saw things he couldn't begin to imagine. Whenever he asked her about it, the answer was always the same: What are you thinking about, Amy? Nothing. Why are you so nervous today, Amy? No reason.

Over the years Jamie had found consolation in the belief that all girls were like that, but he still found it frustrating. In his opinion everything should have a logical explanation, but his sister's behavior often defied explanation. *Facts* were the key to all solutions, he reasoned. Yet at the moment he had no facts. And until he had, whatever was going on at school would remain a perplexing mystery.

When math was over, Jamie couldn't wait to get to gym class. Normally he didn't care much for volleyball, but with outdoor sports activities discontinued, it was better than nothing. With any luck, if he reached the gym early, he could be a forward on Keith Wilcox's team and have a good, competitive game.

Luckily, things went as planned. By the time Mr. Ridgely took attendance, all the boys had chosen up sides. But the gym was in an unusual mess. The first-graders (denied access to the playground) had left jump ropes, beach balls, and other equipment scattered around the floor.

Mr. Ridgely blew his whistle to announce cleanup detail. "Ferguson and Wilcox, clear the floor before the game begins," he said. "Stack everything in the locker, then get out the volleyballs. Hotchkiss and Sumner, you put up the net. Who wants to keep score?"

Nelson Ratner (who hated volleyball) volunteered.

Jamie and Keith quickly picked up all the things from the gym floor and began stacking them in the large equipment locker near the corner wall. On the top shelf were medicine balls, basketballs, and some heavy weight-lifting equipment, which was not generally used. As Jamie hurriedly shoved the toys onto the bottom shelf, he didn't notice the odd creaking sound just above him. Somehow the locker had tilted forward. With the doors still open, the heavy medicine balls and gym equipment could slide forward on the shelves, and at any moment they could crash to the ground, injuring whoever might be in their path.

Meanwhile Amy was in the biology lab. Mr. Slattery was giving a written test on osteology, the science of bones. The school's laboratory skeleton (nicknamed Boney Mahoney) stood in a corner of the room, and Mr. Slattery poked him with a pointer to designate the various types of bones.

"All right, class," he said, "please begin writing. List the bones in the four categories: long, short, flat, and irregular. And proper spelling, please."

Amy was having a rough time, as usual. Apart from being a terrible speller, she always confused the clavicle and the occipital bone, never knowing which was long and which was flat. Staring at the skeleton, she remembered a story her mother had once told her. When Mrs. Ferguson had attended Hillcrest, a clever student had written the names of the bones across the skeleton. Unfortunately, the words had been removed.

Amy sighed. It was no use trying to remember the answers; she didn't know them. She could sit for another fifty years (equally as long as Boney Mahoney had been standing in the corner of the lab) and she still wouldn't know the answers.

"Next come the carpus and the metacarpus," said Mr. Slattery, poking the skeleton again.

Suddenly Amy's eyes became riveted on the skeleton, and a cold chill passed across her body. She realized that at any moment something awful was going to happen in the gym. Staring into space, she pushed back her chair and stood up.

"Amy Ferguson, what's wrong?" asked Mr. Slattery. "If you've finished the answer, go on to the next written question."

"No," she said, "I have to leave." Then she ran from the lab and hurried down the marble corridor toward the gymnasium. She pushed open the door at the very instant the medicine balls and weight-lifting equipment began rolling down the polished floor. The balls hit the net, collapsing it in the center. One barbell kept rolling until it hit Keith Wilcox in the ankles and he fell to the

27

floor. Another crashed into a bench where several boys were seated, knocking them all to the ground.

The mayhem was over before anyone even knew what had happened!

"What was that?" Keith shouted. "An earthquake?"

"Are you okay?" asked Mr. Ridgely.

"I'm not sure," he said, rubbing his ankle.

"You boys better go to the first-aid room and have the nurse check you out."

Amy was still standing in the doorway, watching Jamie pick himself up off the ground. "Are you okay?" she asked.

"I guess so," he said, making certain nothing was broken. "Somebody better fix that dumb locker. We all could've been *killed*. What are you doing in here, anyway?"

"Oh, nothing," she said, "just passing by."

"Well, you look white as a sheet," he noted. "Are you sure you don't want to come to the nurse's room with us?"

"Girls!" grumbled Keith Wilcox. "*Everything* upsets them!"

Before school was dismissed that afternoon, Miss Apthorp made another announcement.

Until further notice, all gym classes were being canceled!

Chapter Five

"WHAT DO YOU THINK OF A COSTUME PARTY?" MRS. FERGUSON asked her husband at dinner that evening. "Wouldn't that make a good fund-raiser?"

"Not if I have to wear tights," he said. "I may teach history, but I don't care to *live* in it; not even for the Historical Society."

"Why must you talk about that?" asked Jamie. "Your fund-raiser is weeks away, but our problem is *now*."

"What problem?" asked his father.

"We're attending an *institution*," Jamie announced dramatically. "Old Appy has turned school into a maximum-security prison, with no time off for good behavior!"

"Yes," said Mrs. Ferguson, "I'd heard Miss Apthorp had canceled several activities. I wonder why?"

"Because someone has a sicko sense of humor, that's why."

"You're wrong," said Amy. "Miss A. closed the gym because the lockers need repair."

"Maybe, but she shouldn't have made such a big deal over a little accident," Jamie argued. "I think she's overreacting."

"But it wasn't an accident," said Amy. She'd blurted out that fact before realizing what she'd said.

Her parents stared at her. "What do you mean, dear?" asked her mother.

Amy didn't know what to say. She knew someone had tampered with the locker shelves. In her mind's eye she could see the tools that had been used to do it. They were wrapped in an old towel and wedged behind the boiler in the basement of Hillcrest. Amy had no idea who had hidden them there, but whoever it was had wanted to frighten the children in the gym. "I mean," she began haltingly, "—well, it wasn't really an accident, was it? Something serious could've happened, but it didn't, did it?"

"*Could have* is quite serious enough," said Mr. Ferguson. "I'm glad Miss Apthorp closed the gym until repairs are made. You'll simply have to grin and bear it, Jamie."

When Jamie entered his sister's room later that night, he wasn't grinning; he was *serious*. "You're hiding something, Amy, and I want to know what it is."

"It's nothing."

"Come off it. You've been keeping secrets from me all

your life and I've put up with it, but this is different. If that business in the gym wasn't an accident, then someone's out to hurt people—including *me*. Say, maybe that falling stage light wasn't accidental either. Maybe someone's trying to *kill* me, for heaven's sake!"

"No, Jamie," she said firmly, "I think somebody's trying to scare *Miss Apthorp*—to get her to close down the school."

"Who would want the school closed? And how do *you* know, anyway?"

"That cabinet was tampered with," she explained. "The front legs were shortened and the brackets were filed down so the equipment would fall out."

"How do you know?"

"I can't tell you."

"Amy, you couldn't know that unless you're mixed up in this."

"No, I *saw* it."

"You did? Then why didn't you tell Mr. Ridgely before all that stuff fell on us? Who'd you see do it?"

Amy hesitated. "No one, exactly. I mean, I didn't actually see it while it was happening—but I knew it was going to happen before it happened."

Jamie was getting annoyed. "What's that mean?"

"Well— I guess you could say I had a vision."

"A *what*?"

Amy regretted having said anything. "Never mind, that's what I call it. You can call it what you like, but don't dare tell anyone about it."

"Tell them *what*?" he asked, totally confused. "I don't

31

understand a word you're saying. Are you trying to tell me you had a *psychic* vision?"

Amy had never used the word *psychic* in her life—not even to herself. It was such an impressive word, with such weighty implications. Psychic people were different, set apart from normal individuals. "I'm not telling you anything. I shouldn't have said anything—I never have before."

"*Before?* You mean this isn't the first time this has happened? Are you telling me you've *always* been psychic?"

Amy felt like kicking herself. The secret she had kept for years was now no longer hidden. What would Jamie think? Would he consider her a freak? "Not always," she replied. "But for a long time I've been able to see things other people can't. I didn't know what it was at first, and I've never really liked it, but there's nothing I can do about it. Most of the time it's an awful feeling. But sometimes it has some advantages, like when I'm playing games."

Jamie had a sudden thought. "*Card* games, for instance? Is that the reason you always beat me, even though I'm a much better player?"

Amy didn't answer.

"Amy, have you been cheating at cards?"

"I *never* cheat," she answered, "but sometimes I can see your hand without looking."

"Oh *really!*"

"That's right, but I can't control what I see. Sometimes I see terrible things I can't do anything about, then at other times— Well, I guess they're things that *might* happen."

32

"You mean like when that stage light fell?" asked Jamie. "Did you see that beforehand?"

"Yes," she admitted. "Just seconds before; that's why I yelled. I had a vision of your body lying underneath the broken glass."

"Then someone *is* trying to kill me!"

"No, Jamie, I think the accident was supposed to *scare* the kids onstage. You couldn't hear the ropes breaking because that scarf was stuffed in your hat. That's why it was only a *maybe* vision, you see?"

Jamie stared at his sister suspiciously. "Are you putting me on, or what?"

Amy knew she'd already said too much. "That's right; I was only fooling."

Confused and skeptical, Jamie tried to reason out the situation. All that Amy had told him about her psychic ability made sense to him, logically speaking. It explained all sorts of behavior he'd wondered about for years; but he still wasn't certain it was true. "What am I thinking right now?" he asked.

"Who knows? I'm not a *mind reader*. Forget what I said, I was only joking."

"No," he said firmly, "I think you were serious. Which means, you *have* been cheating at cards all your life! What a stinking thing to do, Amy Ferguson. Lots of those games had *money* bets. I'll bet you owe me a *fortune*." He started to leave the room. "I'm telling Mom and Dad. They shouldn't have let you get away with this all these years. Someone should've let me in on this deal long ago."

"No, you can't tell Mom and Dad," Amy pleaded, grabbing his arm. "They don't know anything about my powers. I've kept it a secret from them too!"

"You have? *Why?*"

Amy was close to tears. "You don't know what it's like having these pictures inside my head, Jamie. Most of the time I don't like it at all. I've read that lots of people have this power—only, when they *talk* about it everyone starts calling them up for weird reasons—to pick lottery numbers or find dead bodies. Don't you see? Dad would probably take me to the university and make me go through tons of tests. *Please* don't tell them, Jamie. I couldn't stand it if people started thinking I was a *freak*!"

"Well, I can't keep it a secret *forever*," he argued.

"Why not? *I* have! When I was little, I thought *everyone* saw the same things I did. But then I realized that wasn't true; that I was *different*. Oh, Jamie, I don't like being different! Lots of times I hoped *you* were seeing the same things too—but you never have, have you?"

"Of course not. I'm absolutely *normal*!"

"See what I mean," she shouted. "Even *you* think I'm weird!"

"Hold it," Jamie protested. "I didn't mean that. Listen, there's lots of scientific evidence that psychic phenomena may exist, but there's no concrete proof. I'm a logical person, so I need *proof*."

"Such as?"

He thought a moment. "Why do you say that accident in the gym wasn't really an accident?"

"I could see the saw used to shorten the legs on the

34

equipment locker, and the file too. They're wrapped in a towel and hidden behind the boiler at school, but I don't know who put them there."

"Well, at least that's concrete evidence—if it actually exists. Tell you what, tomorrow we'll get to school early and check out the basement."

"Then you do believe me?"

"Maybe I do," he said cautiously, "and maybe I don't."

"I hope there aren't any *rats* down here," said Amy as she and her brother entered the basement of Hillcrest the next morning.

"If you're psychic, you should *know*," Jamie answered, bumping into a rusty unused storage cabinet.

"Quit teasing," she whispered, "can't you see I'm scared? This place is creepy."

The twins couldn't find the light switch, so in the darkness they stumbled past cardboard cartons, cleaning equipment, and discarded school desks.

"There it is." Jamie was now pointing toward the corner beneath the insulated pipes. "Hey, it's ten times bigger than our boiler at home. Where's this stuff supposed to be hidden?"

"Wedged in the back, wrapped in a towel," Amy explained.

Jamie crawled behind the grime-covered boiler. He dragged out a soiled blue towel, unfolded it, and discovered a large saw and two metal files wrapped inside.

"See, I told you," Amy said excitedly. "That's concrete evidence, right?"

"Sure, but of what? You could've hidden this stuff here yourself."

"You don't really believe that, do you?"

"I guess not." Jamie's mind raced toward some logical conclusion. "But if I don't believe you're involved in this, I have to believe you're psychic. And that still doesn't explain why someone's trying to cause accidents at Hillcrest. What's the motive?"

"I've no idea." Amy sighed. "But I'm sure there's danger here. What should we do?"

"I know. Why not go into a trance or something and discover who's doing this stuff?"

"It doesn't work that way, Jamie. I never know when I'm going to see something, and I never know what it'll be."

Jamie was beginning to enjoy the perplexing elements of the situation. "Looks like we've got a real puzzle here. For now, let's leave this stuff where we found it and get up to class. We won't mention anything about it until we have some hard evidence. Whatever's going on here, there has to be a *reason*."

Chapter Six

THE TWINS HURRIED TOWARD THE MAIN ENTRANCE OF HILLCREST, afraid someone might already have noticed they were late for class. As it turned out, there was a huge crowd in the lobby, and the first classes of the day had been delayed. Several of the teachers were trying to maintain order in the midst of total confusion. Many of the first-graders were upset, and a few of the older children were pushing one another. The entire crowd was hovering about the center of the marble entrance hall, below the two-sided grand staircase. Students also hung over the banister, trying to determine what had caused this total focus of attention.

"What's wrong?" asked Jamie. "Did someone faint in the hall or something?"

"I can't see a thing," said Amy, trying to peer over

Linda Grimsby's head. Linda was the tallest girl in school, and standing behind her, Amy felt as if she were being pushed against a *mountain*.

The twins could hear Miss Apthorp's voice rising above the crowd: "Everyone please proceed to your classes. Nothing serious has happened, so don't be alarmed. Teachers, you must maintain *order*."

That was easier said than done. Whatever was causing the furor had definitely upset many of the younger children.

"I'm *scared*," one child moaned tearfully. "I don't like this place anymore."

"Yeah," shouted another, "I wanna go *home*."

Gradually the teachers began to calm the younger students and lead them up the stairs to their classrooms. As the crowd thinned out, the twins finally saw what had caused the disturbance. It was the portrait of Alexander Cartwright, which hung several feet above the mahogany staircase. The huge oil painting had been a permanent fixture at Hillcrest Academy since the day school had opened fifty years earlier. Alexander Cartwright had always hung there regally. Students passed daily beneath his imposing gaze.

But now the portrait looked quite different. The paternal smile had become a vicious leer. The eyes were those of a madman, and the sharp teeth resembled the fangs of a wild animal. It was an evil, wicked face that stared down at the twins—the face of the devil himself! An entirely new expression had been painted onto the picture.

Jamie's mouth hung open. "What *happened*?"

Miss Apthorp tried to remain calm. "Clearly it's another case of vandalism. A cruel practical joke, that's all; but I intend to get to the bottom of it. Until I do, I'm stationing a guard in the entrance lobby during school hours. Now get to your classes, all of you." She dashed up the stairs to her office and closed the door behind her.

Amy stared at her brother. "I told you something terrible was going on."

Jamie nodded. "But it's not ordinary vandalism. No kid could've defaced that painting. It's hanging up fifteen feet high. A person would need a ten-foot ladder just to reach it."

"You're right," Amy said. "Oh, I wish I could figure out what's happening."

"I know one thing," Jamie said. "Miss Apthorp is hiding something. She knows much more about this deal than she's letting on."

"What makes you think so?"

"Logic. Appy had a *fit* when that cake was messed up, but that was minor. Now this is *major vandalism* and she's trying to pretend it's nothing."

"Well, maybe she's trying not to frighten us."

"Could be, but she's frightened herself, I can tell. Amy, I'm telling you, she definitely *knows something*."

For the remainder of the day Hillcrest Academy truly seemed like a prison. Following Miss Apthorp's instructions, all classroom doors were locked during each period. Students needed special permission to go to the bathroom. Teachers had to give up their study periods to stand guard in the hallways. Lunch trays were brought to the rooms, and students were denied access to the cafeteria.

By two o'clock many children had begun calling the school by its new nickname, "the Rock." Several pretended they were dragging a ball and chain behind them as they walked through the halls.

"Three o'clock had better come soon," said Ira Canfield. "My parents will probably have to put up *bail* to get me out of here!"

Amy failed to see the humor in the situation. She had the unsettling feeling that things were even *worse* than she'd imagined. She tried concentrating on the identity of the culprit, hoping a picture might float into her mind— but nothing came. For the first time in her life she actually *wanted* a psychic vision, but she couldn't manage one. It was very frustrating.

Jamie, on the other hand, seemed stimulated by the bewildering occurrences. He had a puzzle to solve, and this he found exhilarating. He was determined to get to the bottom of the mystery—personally.

At three o'clock when school let out, the special security guard Miss Apthorp had hired was standing in the main lobby. Someone had draped a large sheet over the disfigured portrait of Alexander Cartwright.

"Miss A. can't cover things up that easily," said Jamie. "I still say she's hiding something."

"A *guard*?" asked Mr. Ferguson at dinner. "That sounds serious."

40

"I don't like it, Richard," said Mrs. Ferguson. "Do you suppose the twins could be in danger?"

"Don't overreact, Miriam. Whoever is playing these sick jokes is bound to stop now. I'll bet by tomorrow Hillcrest will be back to normal."

It wasn't. Despite all Miss Apthorp's precautions, terrible things were still happening.

The next morning a brief, ominous message was scrawled across the blackboard in Mr. Duval's French classroom: MORT.

The younger students couldn't decipher its meaning, but Mr. Duval didn't have to tell the older students that *mort* meant *"death"*!

At ten o'clock several classes were in the library for study period. Students were reading quietly while Mrs. Camden, the librarian, cataloged new books. Suddenly a strange, unearthly cry broke through the silence.

The twins, seated at a corner table, glanced up and stared at each other. What was it?

Mrs. Camden glanced up too.

The cry had started out softly but quickly changed to an eerie moan which filled the entire room. It was a horribly sad groan, like a voice traveling from the dead.

Mrs. Camden tapped her pencil on the desk. "Who's doing that? Stop it at once!"

It didn't stop.

The sound grew louder and louder until the children were forced to cover their ears. Then several of the little ones began to cry.

"I'm scared, Mrs. Camden," sobbed Wendy Vernon. "What's happening?"

"Something must be wrong with the intercom," explained Mrs. Camden. "I'll speak to Miss Apthorp about it."

Later that morning Miss Apthorp closed the library until further notice.

At midday all the coats in the cloakroom on the main floor were found scattered along the marble entrance hall. They'd been slashed to pieces.

Miss Apthrop ordered the cloakroom closed until further notice.

Freddie the custodian, always the voice of doom, went shuffling around the school, picking things up, cleaning, and doing repairs. He grumbled his usual comment: "Children don't belong in a place like this."

The twins were beginning to agree.

"What kind of sick person wants to scare kids?" asked Jamie.

Suddenly the thought came to Amy. It wasn't a person, after all. Rather, some strange force had been unleashed within the school. "A supernatural force," she told Jamie.

"That's crazy," said her brother. "I still say everything that's happened has a logical explanation."

But by that afternoon things had begun to defy logic!

* * *

At two-fifteen both seventh-grade classes were in the biology lab, and Mr. Slattery was reviewing the material that he'd covered that week.

"Now, class, a few words about the cranial region," he said, directing his pointer toward the skeleton's head. "This is the occipitofrontalis. It consists of two muscular slips separated by—"

Heidi Wentworth let out a sudden, bloodcurdling scream. "Look at the skeleton," she cried, "he's *moving*."

Dumbstruck, the entire class stared at Boney Mahoney. They heard a strange creaking sound as his skull began to turn from side to side. Then he raised his arm, stepped forward on his skeletal feet, and began to approach the children.

Mr. Slattery was as surprised as everyone else. "What on earth . . ."

"I'm getting out of here," shouted Robert Teasdale as he rushed toward the door. "This school is *jinxed* or something!"

"Calm down," Mr. Slattery pleaded. "There must be some reasonable explanation for this."

No one listened. The students had already heard too many logical explanations, none of which made sense, and within moments they were stampeding toward the door. Mr. Slattery was forced to unlock it.

The noise and confusion of fifty students spilling out into the hall all at once didn't go unnoticed. The other teachers began unlocking their doors and poking their heads out.

"Boney Mahoney is *alive*," the children shouted.

43

Miss Apthorp came hurrying down the hall. "That's ridiculous, children."

Mr. Slattery quickly locked the door of the biology lab, to keep Boney Mahoney from escaping. He'd hoped that might bring an end to the chaos in the hall, but it didn't. By now all the teachers were confused, frightened, and frustrated.

"Something strange is going on here," said Mr. Duval.

"Something serious," said Mr. Ridgely.

"And the children are definitely not safe," added Mrs. Camden.

"I'm getting out of here," whined Cindy Solomon, "and I'm never coming back."

Miss Apthorp, looking strained and haggard, blew a stray wisp of gray hair over her forehead and sighed. "I'm afraid you're right; this is serious. I now have no other choice. I'm officially closing Hillcrest until further notice!"

Chapter Seven

WHEN MR. FERGUSON RETURNED FROM HIS HISTORY CLASS, THE twins told him the news. "Closed the school?" he asked. "But Miss Apthorp can't do that."

"She said it was necessary, Richard," his wife explained. "There've been several more strange events, and no one knows who's responsible. I certainly don't want the twins placed in any danger."

"Neither do I, Miriam, but there must be some—"

"Logical explanation," interrupted Jamie. "That's what I've been saying, Dad."

"Well, until it's discovered," said his mother, "you children will have to be enrolled at Westlake Elementary."

"Westlake?" Amy groaned. "I don't want to go *there*. Sarah Dudley goes there and I hate Sarah Dudley. We'll probably wind up in the same class and I'll have to sit next to her and she'll begin teasing me the way she always did when we were little and— "

"I'm calling Miss Apthorp," said her father. "This whole thing makes absolutely no sense!"

Amy slumped on the sofa, looking solemn. There was no way she would attend Westlake, she told herself. Since the age of three she'd hated Sarah Dudley, and she refused to sit next to her in any classroom in the *world*, and that was that.

If only she could figure out what was happening at Hillcrest! Amy tried concentrating on the face of the unknown person who had hidden those tools behind the boiler. In her mind's eye all she saw was the hideous sight of Boney Mahoney moving toward her. His arms were outstretched, as if he were pleading with her for help. It frightened her so, she closed her eyes and the vision was gone.

"That poor woman has been on the phone all evening," said Mr. Ferguson, returning to the room. "Every parent has been calling her for information."

Mrs. Ferguson wasn't surprised. "Naturally. She can't close down the school arbitrarily."

"She's having an engineering inspection performed," he explained. "That may take several days. Miss Apthorp feels that since the building is so old, there may be some structural weakness."

"That's stupid," said Jamie. "Besides, it doesn't explain ripped-up coats, the destruction of the portrait, or all the other creepy things."

"True," agreed his father. "But Miss Apthorp feels

46

there's also a sadistic prankster on the loose. Once the building is closed, she hopes he'll discontinue these idiotic practical jokes. After talking with her, I see she has little choice in the matter. Whatever the reason, Hillcrest isn't safe just now."

"But Hillcrest has *never* been closed," said Mrs. Ferguson, obviously upset. "And I can't think who would want to play such a dreadful joke on anyone."

"Neither can I, Miriam. But for now it looks like the twins will *have* to go to Westlake Elementary."

Suddenly Amy could see Sarah Dudley's putrid face staring at her, and she could hear the nasty comments Sarah could always be relied upon to make. But it wasn't a psychic vision: it was grim reality.

Later that evening Heidi Wentworth's mother called Mrs. Ferguson. "Is that you, Miriam? I'm so upset, I can't tell you. Enrollment at Westlake is *closed*. So many parents called to transfer their children, they've run out of space. They hope to have sufficient desks and chairs for students in another week or so. Until then our children have no place to go."

Amy was thrilled: a last-minute reprieve.

"Don't look so smug, young lady," said her father. "It seems fate has given you kids a brief vacation, but it won't last long. In a few days you'll be going to school *somewhere*."

"Sabotage." Jamie was thinking out loud as he rocked on the porch swing after dinner. He stared out at the darkness through the trees, listening to nature's familiar night sounds.

Amy was rocking, too, as she stared out into the night in silence. "What'd you say?"

"Sabotage," he repeated. "That's what's going on at school. But *why*? There has to be a *motive*."

Jamie could see his sister's face turn suddenly grim under the porch light. He noticed that expression she always had when her mind seemed to wander.

"I think it's supernatural," she said solemnly, "and the skeleton has something to do with it."

"That's stupid, Amy. I don't care if you're psychic or not, that's plain stupid. The motive is either revenge, jealousy, or profit." As always, Jamie's mind was functioning logically. "I don't think Miss A. has ever done anything mean enough to warrant revenge, so that's out. And jealousy usually involves a jealous lover, so that's definitely out. Which leaves profit. Somehow, someone will be richer if Miss Apthorp has to close down the school for good."

Amy heard a strange rustling sound in the apple trees, and a chill ran through her. "I'm telling you, it's supernatural."

"Look, Amy, do you want to help me in this deal or not? If we don't solve this mystery, Hillcrest will *never* reopen and you'll be at Westlake, with Sarah Dudley staring down your nose."

"How can *I* help?"

"Are you sure you haven't had any more fits or trances?"

"I don't get fits or trances; I *see* things. But all I've seen lately is that *skeleton*, so that's why I think—"

48

"It's supernatural. Yeah, I know."

"I still want to help," she added, "but I don't know how."

"Well, I do. We're going to investigate this case on our own."

"How?"

"We can put our time to good use, since there's no school for a few days. Let's go down to the *Monroe Gazette* and check through some old newspapers, okay? Maybe we could speak with the editor, Emile Bruckner. I'll bet he knows everything and everyone in this town. If there are any clues to be found, we might find them there."

Amy tossed about restlessly that night. She was uncertain whether she was dreaming or having a peculiar hallucination. There seemed to be a strange light by the foot of her bed. The light suddenly transformed itself into a human shape that glowed like a flame, illuminating the room. Something, she felt, was pulling her toward the apparition. Amy sat up in bed and found herself staring into darkness. Then a strange vibration traveled through her body, and she fell asleep.

Immediately after breakfast the next morning Mrs. Ferguson buried herself beneath a pile of papers she had dragged down from the attic. She had decided an auction might be the wisest fund-raiser for the Historical Society and was hoping to unearth something of value from among her grandfather's belongings.

Mr. Ferguson suggested the twins go along with him to Monroe University and spend the day in the library. "Just because there's no school doesn't mean you can't learn something."

"Oh, we'll learn something," said Jamie. "We're going to the *Gazette* this morning to interview the editor. Me and Amy thought that might make a good extra-credit project, isn't that right?"

Amy nodded. She was still disturbed about the strange dream she'd had the night before. What did it mean? she wondered.

"You're interviewing Emile Bruckner?" her father asked. "Good. That'll keep you out of trouble for the day."

Several typewriters were clicking away in unison as the twins entered the offices of the *Monroe Gazette*.

"We'd like to speak with the editor," said Jamie. "It's very important."

A young reporter glanced up from his desk. "He's awfully busy right now. What's it about?"

"A school project," Amy explained. "We need information."

"I can't guarantee he'll talk to you, but that's his office over there."

Mr. Bruckner's "office" was a glass-enclosed cubby in the corner. Stacked in messy piles along his desk were papers, files, phone books, half-finished cups of coffee, and half-eaten doughnuts. Emile Bruckner was huddled somewhere in the center, underneath a cloud of smelly cigar smoke. "What can I do for you kids?"

"We'd like to see some mug shots of practical jokers," said Amy.

Grinning, Mr. Bruckner blew a stinky smoke ring in her direction. "Mug shots? This isn't the police station, kid. Even if it was, they don't have mug shots either. This is Monroe County, not New York City. What do you want with mug shots, anyway?"

"That's not what we want," Jamie answered. "We're researching the history of Hillcrest Academy."

"Hillcrest? Oh yeah, funny things have been going on there lately. I hear Jemima Apthorp just closed the place down. I sent a reporter out there yesterday, but she wouldn't talk about it."

"*We* will," said Jamie. "If you help us, we'll give you an exclusive story."

Mr. Bruckner chuckled. "Exclusive, eh? Kid, this is the only paper in town; *everything's* exclusive. What do you want to know?"

"Whatever there is to know about Hillcrest," Jamie explained. "Could you tell us something about the property or Alexander Cartwright? Was there ever a scandal out there or anything?"

Bruckner scratched his head. "Well, there was that business with the Cartwright boy, but that was way back—almost fifty years ago. I was just a green cub reporter then, but I remember it. Old man Cartwright had the cops chasing that kid all over the state, but they never found him."

"I didn't know Alexander Cartwright had a *son*," said Amy.

"Oh, sure. What was his name again? Albert. Yeah, he was a bad one, always in a mess of trouble. Just goes to show you, right? With all the dough Cartwright had, he couldn't buy himself a decent son."

"Why were the police after him?" asked Jamie. "Was he a criminal?"

"Oh, Albert was always in trouble. Then he suddenly disappeared one day—left town without a word and was never seen again. Cartwright had the police on his trail forever, though they never found him. But the old man never gave up hope he might return someday. Funny, isn't it? If Albert had hung around, he could've been a millionaire. Instead, old Cartwright gave everything to charity. Except Hillcrest, of course. Albert still possibly owns that."

"What do you mean?" asked Jamie. "I thought Miss Apthorp owned Hillcrest."

"Well—yes and no," Mr. Bruckner answered. "Technically, the town owns it. Miss Apthorp merely leases the property for the sum of one dollar a year. See, according to Cartwright's will, if Hillcrest doesn't remain a school, it reverts back to the Cartwright estate for one year. After that, if no living relative claims the property, Monroe County can claim ownership."

Jamie was convinced this was the solid evidence he'd been searching for. "So Albert Cartwright could still be alive!"

"I guess so," Mr. Bruckner said. "As far as I can figure, he'd be around my age. No spring chicken, that's for sure."

"No kidding?" Jamie said excitedly. "Well, maybe you've seen him hanging around town?"

Emile Bruckner threw his cigar butt into his coffee cup. "Maybe I see him twice a day, but I'd never know it. Albert Cartwright was only a kid when he left Monroe. Who knows what he looks like *now*?"

"That's right, he could be *anyone*," said Jamie. As he stared out the window of the *Gazette* office, he noticed an old man strolling down Main Street, outside the Ice Cream Parlor. A stranger in town? he wondered. Could he be Albert Cartwright, back in Monroe to claim his inheritance?

Amy also glanced out the window, and she, too, grew excited. "Look, there's that man—the one who was in Miss Apthorp's office the other day." The stranger no longer had his jacket collar pulled up to his face, but he still looked suspicious. "Mr. Bruckner, do you know that man talking with Mr. Hennessy out there?"

Bruckner glanced out the window. "Sure, that's Harold Metcalfe. He's the new member of the town's planning commission. Why'd you ask?"

"He was at Hillcrest the other day," explained Amy. "Whatever he told Miss Apthorp really upset her, so I thought that maybe. . . ."

"I see what you're thinking," said Mr. Bruckner. "You figure *he* might be Albert Cartwright, back to claim his inheritance. Sorry, kids, Metcalfe isn't old enough. He's only in his forties. But I'm sure Miss Apthorp was probably upset by his visit. See, he's been pressuring the planning commission to have the Hillcrest property re-

53

zoned. Metcalfe is in real estate and he has some big idea about building condos on that property."

"But he can't do that, can he?" asked Jamie.

"No, not as long as Miss Apthorp runs Hillcrest. But she's not a young woman. If she decides to retire and no one else agrees to take over, I guess it could happen."

In Jamie's mind pieces of the puzzle were suddenly clicking into place. "Thanks for your time, Mr. Bruckner, you've been very helpful."

"No trouble, just don't forget my 'exclusive.' If you kids figure out what's going on at Hillcrest, it'll be front-page news."

"You'll be the first to know, I promise," said Jamie. Nudging Amy to follow, he hurriedly left the office of the *Monroe Gazette*.

"It finally makes sense, don't you see?" said Jamie as they walked down Main Street. "I told you the motive was profit. Metcalfe stands to make a fortune if Hillcrest closes. He can put up dozens of condo apartments on that property. But first he needs to frighten Miss A. into closing the school. So far he's done a pretty good job. No one's going to send their kids to a school they think is *jinxed*."

Amy still felt there was an element to the mystery neither one of them could comprehend, and she couldn't shake her feeling that the *skeleton* had something to do with it. "Even if you're right, it still doesn't make any sense. Hillcrest won't close unless Albert Cartwright is alive to claim his property."

"Then they're in it *together*. It's a conspiracy between Cartwright and Metcalfe to get Miss A. to close Hillcrest permanently."

"But we've no proof that Albert Cartwright is alive, Jamie. Even if he is, we don't know *who* he is."

"Maybe not, but I've got a strong suspicion. C'mon, Amy, we're going out to Hillcrest right now."

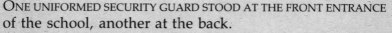

Chapter Eight

ONE UNIFORMED SECURITY GUARD STOOD AT THE FRONT ENTRANCE of the school, another at the back.

"We'll never *get in.*" Amy glanced at the two men from behind the trees surrounding the property.

"Yes, we will," said Jamie. "We left the basement door unlocked yesterday, remember? I'll bet it's still open."

Jamie began throwing rocks toward the windows of the front entrance to divert the guards' attention.

"Hey, Larry," one guard shouted to the other, "there's someone hiding in those bushes."

As the men rushed to investigate, the twins scurried toward the basement entrance of the building. They entered quickly.

"Now what?" asked Amy breathlessly.

"We get evidence, of course. First, we'll take those

tools hidden behind the boiler. They might have some fingerprints on them. If Albert Cartwright was ever arrested, there'll be a record of his prints."

"Good thinking," said Amy as she watched her brother retrieve the towel from behind the boiler. "But be *quiet*. If that guard hears us down here, we're in big trouble."

"There's probably lots more clues hidden around here. Sure, look at that," he said, pointing toward the ladder propped against the wall. "I'll bet that was used to reach the portrait in the lobby. See, we're finally getting somewhere." Jamie began rifling through storage cabinets and moving things around on shelves.

"There are lots of trunks stacked back here," Amy whispered from the corner. "I'll check through them."

The basement of Hillcrest Academy had a dual purpose. It was used to store unused school equipment and maintenance supplies, and it also held dozens of boxes filled with memorabilia Alexander Cartwright had collected in his travels, things that hadn't been sold at auction.

The rusty hinges of an old steamer trunk squeaked as Amy raised the lid. She gasped when she saw what was inside. Beady eyes and savage teeth stared back at her. It took a minute for her to realize that whatever dreadful creature resided within the trunk, it wasn't alive but was *stuffed*.

"How disgusting," she said, quickly closing the lid. "It's a stuffed monkey. I wonder how long the poor thing's been in there."

Jamie unearthed a box filled with grotesque carved masks. "Cartwright must've been a real weirdo."

"Jamie, I think we're getting off the scent."

"You're right, we won't find any clues in this junk." Stumbling over the boxes and cartons, Jamie came upon something hidden in a corner. "Hey look, a tape recorder." He switched it on, and the twins heard the eerie moaning sound that had filled the library the day before. "Clever, eh? I'll bet this tape was hooked up to the intercom system. This whole thing is definitely an inside job. And I'll bet the guy responsible for it all is— "

Jamie stopped in midsentence, as he heard footsteps coming down the basement stairs. "Let's get out of sight," he whispered.

Quickly the twins hurried toward the storage room at the rear of the basement and closed the door behind them. Their hearts beat faster as they stood huddled in a corner beside the mops and pails. Amy bumped her head on the naked light bulb dangling from the ceiling. "Don't make a sound," Jamie whispered. "This guy is dangerous and means business."

Amy's voice trembled: "Who?"

"Albert Cartwright, of course. That's not what he calls himself, but that's who he is."

The twins froze. The footsteps had stopped directly outside the storage room door. As Amy pressed her back tighter against the wall, an old photo album fell to the ground from its resting place on the shelf above her head. She panicked for a second, afraid the man outside the door had heard it fall.

They stood in silence as they heard a coin being dropped into the payphone on the basement wall.

"I'll bet he's calling his accomplice," Jamie whispered.

"You still haven't told me who you think it is."

"How come *you're* psychic but *I* have all the answers? It's Freddie the custodian, of course."

Amy was about to argue it couldn't possibly be cranky old Freddie, when the voice began to speak into the phone—and then she knew it *was*.

"Yeah, things are fine here, Mr. Metcalfe," said Freddie. "Everything's going according to plan. . . . No, I'm not worried about that engineering inspection. When they learn there's nothing structurally wrong with this place, everyone in town will be convinced it's jinxed or haunted. No kid'll ever set foot in here again. . . . Listen, don't worry, I plan to ditch the wig and overalls soon. Then I'll look like a new person. . . . Yeah, right, it's just a matter of time now. Pretty soon this property will be mine and we can make a fortune on it."

After Freddie hung up the phone, the twins heard his footsteps gradually retreat down the basement hall.

"What'd I tell you?" said Jamie. "Now we've got concrete evidence that Freddie is actually Albert Cartwright."

"Should we go to the police now?" asked Amy.

"I guess so. But first, let's call Miss Apthorp and have her meet us at the police station. Maybe she can swear out a warrant for Freddie's arrest."

Chapter Nine

MISS APTHORP WAS OBVIOUSLY ANNOYED. "YOU CERTAINLY HAVE some explaining to do, children. Why on earth did you insist I meet you both here?"

Police Chief Emory offered her a seat. "Take it easy, ma'am. These kids seem to feel they've solved the mystery that's going on out at your school."

"There's nothing going on out there," she said defensively. "Just silly nonsense and superstition aggravated by some prankster. But believe me, I've the situation well in hand."

Jamie was certain Miss Apthorp's total denial of the problem was her feeble attempt to protect her school. "We know Mr. Metcalfe has been threatening you. That's who you're frightened of, isn't it? He's the one responsible for all this trouble, isn't he?"

"Nonsense," said Miss Apthorp indignantly. But then she removed a handkerchief from her purse and suddenly began to sob into it. "All right, I admit it. I can't stand this tension any longer. Mr. Metcalfe threatened to hurt the children if I said anything. At first I didn't take him seriously. Then when strange things began happening, I instituted safety measures to protect my students, but you can't keep children locked in their classrooms indefinitely! Mr. Metcalfe left me no choice; I *had* to close the school. I was hoping to reopen at a later date, but now I realize no one will ever again want their youngsters to attend Hillcrest. Many parents think the building is *haunted*."

Police Chief Emory scratched his head. "What does Mr. Metcalfe have to do with this?"

The twins quickly filled him in on all the information they'd gathered, and also explained how Freddie the custodian was involved in the scheme. "He's actually Albert Cartwright in disguise," said Jamie.

"This is a very serious allegation," said the police chief. "What evidence do you kids have?"

"Freddie's fingerprints are probably on these tools. He used them to tamper with the equipment locker," explained Amy.

Emory wasn't impressed. "Why shouldn't they be? After all, he's the school custodian; they're *his* tools."

Jamie was getting annoyed. "Can't you at least call him in for questioning?"

Emory nodded. "Sure, but I can't arrest him without evidence." The police chief called in an officer. "Filby, drive by the Monroe Arms and bring Fred Bascombe back here for questioning."

Miss Apthorp, controlling her tears, seemed confused. "What makes you think our custodian is actually Albert Cartwright? I always assumed Albert had died years ago. He was such an unpleasant young man, I *knew* he'd wind up badly, but I never thought. . . ."

"You *knew* him?" asked Jamie.

"Oh, yes," said Miss Apthorp. "As young people, we attended many social functions together. I remember one especially lovely catered picnic on the grounds of the estate. It was spring and the magnolia trees were in full bloom."

"I hope you kids haven't gotten me involved in a wild-goose chase," said Chief Emory. "If Miss Apthorp remembers Albert Cartwright and she doesn't recognize Freddie to be Albert, then he can't be the same person."

"Oh, but that was ages ago," explained Miss Apthorp. "If only I'd kept a photograph of him as a young man, I might've been able to make the connection and see the resemblance."

Emory shrugged. "Well, I don't think he'll oblige us with a snapshot."

Miss Apthorp tried to recall the young Albert Cartwright. Was there some specific mannerism of his that reminded her of Freddie?

Amy was thinking too. In her mind's eye she focused in on something she knew was important. It had something to do with snapshots. Yes, that was it; there were several snapshots in the storage cabinet down in the basement at Hillcrest. She remembered the photo album that had fallen on her head while they were hiding. Amy could see the pictures on all the pages—snapshots of Albert Cartwright at the picnic Miss Apthorp had mentioned. There was one of Albert in a pin-stripe suit and bowler hat and smiling at the camera—and it definitely resembled Freddie.

"Officer Filby is bringing in Bascombe for interrogation," Emory explained, "but we can't hold him long without charging him with something. And we can't charge him without proof."

"We have proof," Amy said excitedly. "We left it at school."

"We did?" asked Jamie.

Amy nudged him. "Sure. We left it in the basement, remember? Gee, that's right, I forgot—only *I* know where it is."

Jamie stared at his sister, totally confused. Then suddenly he realized she must have received some psychic clue. "Sure, the *proof*. Yeah, we'll go get it right now."

"Go where?" asked Emory.

"Out to Hillcrest."

"That's not safe. I'll send an officer along with you. Hey, I can't do that; I just sent my last man out to pick up Bascombe."

"I've an idea," said Jamie. "Write us a note to give the security guard and he'll let us in."

"Okay," Emory agreed, "but you'd better come back with some hard evidence. I can't stall Bascombe for long."

*   *   *

63

"We have to hurry," said Jamie, glancing around the basement. "The guard said he'd only allow us ten minutes in here. Where's that album you told me about?"

Amy pointed toward the storage closet. "There are lots of snapshots of Albert Cartwright in that album, and one of them looks just like Freddie, only much younger."

Jamie hurried toward the closet, snatched the album from the floor, and quickly turned the pages. "You're right, Amy. If you gave this guy some wrinkles, a white wig, and some overalls, it would look just like Freddie. Great, now we've got real evidence." Jamie heard a sound on the stairs above. "That's probably the guard coming to get us; let's go."

Amy heard the strange clattering on the stairs, but somehow she knew it wasn't the guard's footsteps at all. It was something ominous and otherworldly, and it was intent on pursuing them.

She gasped. The shadow of the skeleton was descending the stairs.

The bones made a dreadful clinking-clanking rattle on the steps. The empty eye sockets stared unseeingly, and the teeth were fixed in a frightening leer. Raising skeletal arms, Boney Mahoney moved in the children's direction.

The twins froze in fear. "I told you there was something supernatural about this," said Amy, her voice quivering with terror.

"Don't be silly," said Jamie, still thinking logically. "It's just another one of Freddie's tricks. He's rigged up some remote-control device to animate the skeleton."

"No, Jamie, Boney Mahoney is *alive* and he's trying to tell us something."

"Well, I don't want to hear it!" The photo album in one hand, Jamie grabbed his sister's arm with the other. Boney Mahoney was now several feet away from them but was getting closer by the moment. Luckily the twins were near enough to the exit to make a quick dash for it. They slammed the heavy metal door behind them. "That'll fix him," said Jamie, breathing a sigh of relief.

Amy sucked in some fresh air and tried to get hold of herself. "You can't stop supernatural forces that easily."

"Will you quit it? You're giving me the creeps. I'm telling you, this is just another one of Freddie's pranks."

They could still hear the skeleton clanking inside, as if he were pounding on the metal door, trying to break free. After a moment the sound stopped, and they heard the bones slump to the floor.

"Is everything okay?" asked the security guard, moving toward the basement entrance.

"Sure, everything's fine," said Jamie. "Just be sure to keep this door locked—no matter what!"

The guard glanced at the door quizzically.

The twins hurried off the grounds of Hillcrest, and made their way back to the police station.

"You can't hold me here," Freddie protested. "I haven't done anything wrong."

The twins dropped the photo album onto Police Chief Emory's desk.

65

"Look at those snapshots," said Jamie. "They're proof Freddie is actually Albert Cartwright."

Emory glanced through the album, then handed it to Miss Apthorp. "My goodness," she said, "I would never have believed it. Yes, now I see the resemblance. Why, of all the . . ." She glanced at her custodian with rage in her eyes. "You miserable creature, how dare you try to destroy my school? You were always a nasty, spiteful individual. I remember you as a young man, Albert, and you were *never* any good!"

"Oh, shut up, you old fool," he shouted. "What if I *am* Albert Cartwright, so what? It's not against the law to change your name. You've no proof I've done anything illegal."

"But we have," said Emory, holding up a sheet of paper. "I put an APB on the wire about you earlier, and we've come up with some interesting information. You're wanted in New York for car theft, in Massachusetts for fraud, and in Illinois for burglary. Even if we can't pin anything on you here, it looks like you'll be spending the rest of your life in jail *somewhere*. You've got charges pending in three states!"

Freddie knew when he was cornered. "Okay, so you've got me nailed. But this whole scheme wasn't my idea, you know. Metcalfe is the guy responsible. I didn't even know I still had legal rights to Hillcrest until he got in touch with me. Him and his big condo idea! I should've known it would turn out to be a bust, just like everything else."

"Don't worry," Emory said. "Metcalfe will be charged as well. I have an officer out right now, picking him up."

Freddie shrugged. "So what if I spend the rest of my life in jail? I've spent most of it there, anyway. Jail is better than this one-horse hick town any day."

Miss Apthorp was furious. "You really are a dreadful man! And after all your dear father tried to do for you."

"*Can* it, lady, will you? One more day out at your school with all those screaming kids would've driven me nuts! At least I *scared* a few of them pretty good, didn't I?" He chuckled to himself.

"You scared them *all*," Miss Apthorp shouted. "You destroyed your father's portrait, sabotaged the gym, and frightened everyone out of their wits."

"And don't forget the skeleton," Jamie added. "You sure managed some clever tricks. That last one nearly scared *us* to death."

"What do you mean?" Freddie asked. "I didn't monkey around with the skeleton."

"Don't deny it," Jamie said. "You rigged up those bones so that they'd move."

"Look, kid," Freddie said angrily. "I'm not talking anymore, see. I said what I said, and that's all I'm gonna say."

The police chief saw no reason to pursue the point. "Either way, we've got enough charges against you. I'm booking you for disorderly conduct until you can be extradited for some of these more serious crimes."

Miss Apthorp was relieved and grateful. "Thanks to you children, Hillcrest is safe again."

67

The twins stared at each other uneasily. Everyone else seemed to think the case was solved, but they knew better. There was no reason for Freddie to lie any longer, so he must have been telling the truth when he said he hadn't touched the skeleton . . . which meant Hillcrest still wasn't safe.

One mystery may have been over, but there was an even bigger puzzle yet unsolved—a *supernatural* one.

Who was Boney Mahoney, and why was he haunting the school?

Chapter Ten

MRS. FERGUSON WAS THRILLED. "I'M SO PROUD OF YOU both!"

"Darn good police work," agreed Mr. Ferguson.

The twins sat in silence, poking at their dinner. All afternoon people had called to congratulate them: together they had solved the puzzle at Hillcrest. Emile Bruckner said it would be front-page news the next day, and Miss Apthorp had plans for a special assembly at which they would be formally congratulated. In spite of all the praise, the twins had maintained their peculiar silence.

"You certainly don't seem overjoyed by all this," observed Mrs. Ferguson.

"I know the problem," said Mr. Ferguson. "You kids don't want to return to school next week. I'll bet you were hoping for a longer vacation, right? Well, even celebrities have to go to school. I thank goodness your school is safe again."

Neither Amy nor Jamie said one word. At that moment their thoughts were identical: The skeleton was still waiting for them in the basement.

"Maybe Freddie *lied* after all." Jamie spoke as he and his sister washed the dinner dishes.

"No, he told us the truth," Amy said solemnly. "That skeleton will still be haunting Hillcrest next week when we return—unless we figure out what he wants."

"Then we'll have to *tell* someone about it, Amy."

"No! If we do, I'd have to tell people I'm psychic, and I won't do that."

Disgusted, Jamie threw the dish towel on the rack. "Well, I'm going to bed. Whatever happens, let's worry about it tomorrow!"

Amy stared out the window toward the row of apple trees in the yard. Dusk had gone, and darkness had fallen. For a moment she thought she saw a strange spectral shape float past the window. At first it seemed merely a light, but then it seemed to form itself into a face. She blinked and it was gone. "I'm going to bed too." She sighed. "Maybe all this will make more sense in the morning."

Amy wasn't certain whether she was asleep or awake. If she was asleep, it seemed a restless slumber; but if she was awake, something strange was definitely occurring.

The room was dark yet filled with light, and the light had an energy surrounding it. That energy seemed to pull her toward a dim specter by the foot of her bed. Somehow, it looked like a puzzle with all its pieces coming together to form the shape of a man. Yes, it was a man in some strange out-of-date uniform, complete with knee britches, epaulets, powdered wig, and sword. The figure was now fully visible; it leaned over the bed with arms outstretched to Amy.

"This is no dream," she said aloud, sitting up in bed, "this is *real*." Fear suddenly took hold of Amy, and she grabbed the lamp by her bedside and threw it at the intruder. She stared in amazement: the lamp seemed to go directly through his body and yet not touch it.

"What do you want?" she screamed. "Are you a burglar?"

Amy could now see the stranger's face clearly; he was frowning. "That's a fine greeting, Cousin," he said in a voice that seemed to come from everywhere yet nowhere, as if it were traveling through an eternal tunnel. "There's no cause to distress yourself. In my day such an antagonistic action would evoke an extreme reprimand. Is this what generations of mollycoddling has produced in the Tredwells?"

"Are you real or a dream?" she asked. "What do you want?"

"I am both real and an illusion," he explained. "I require assistance and also offer it."

Amy blinked. In the past, visions would always go away when she blinked, but this one didn't. When she opened her eyes again, the stranger was still standing by her bed.

"Is this some psychic vision or a nightmare?" she asked.

"Your awareness shall reveal what is truth and what is not." The stranger drew closer. "Child, attend me. You possess a gift to which we must address ourselves."

"Then this *is* a vision?" asked Amy. She wasn't at all certain she wouldn't prefer a burglar. "Who are you and what do you want? Are you the same shape that appeared outside the kitchen window earlier?"

"I am. Through winters and summers you may find me here, for it is where I choose to be."

"Well, I've never seen you before. At least I don't think so, unless it was in a dream. I certainly would've remembered that outfit."

The apparition seemed to take that as a compliment. "My garb pleases you, then? Yes, I wore it nobly in my lifetime and choose to retain it in my afterlife."

Amy shuddered. "Your *afterlife*? You mean you're *dead*?"

"Such a word is meaningless. Hark ye, child, for I have come with a distinct purpose. Do not be in such a fluster, I mean you no harm."

"But I've never met a *ghost* before."

The spirit moved still closer. "I entreat you to listen. My appearance should not upset you, now that you have acknowledged your psychic gifts. This power enables you to realize that all time exists concurrently. One needs only to be able to see this as such."

"No, I don't see anything," said Amy, "except that I'm talking to a ghost and I'm *scared*."

The spirit seemed to grow annoyed. "Do not be so insolent. Spirit I may be, but kin I am as well. You have the word of a soldier and a gentleman that my mission is upstanding. Upon my honor."

"Kin? Does that mean you're some kind of *relative*?"

"Good, I see you have a brain. But questions serve no purpose. I am here to request your aid, and I must attain it before disaster befalls many."

"My aid? How can I help a ghost?"

The apparition sat at the foot of the bed, and Amy watched, fascinated. His body made no indentation on the coverlet.

"Firstly, remove that word from your vocabulary," he continued. "The very sound of it gives me the collywobbles. If you must address me in such a manner, refer to me as a spirit. Now, in reference to your query, I entreat your assistance in assuaging the forces that are presently active within Hillcrest. Supernatural forces."

"Supernatural?" Amy repeated. "Do you mean the skeleton at school? What do *you* know about Boney Mahoney? Please, tell me what's going on!"

The spirit suddenly stood up. In military fashion he clasped the sword by his side. "Calm yourself, child. Remember you are a Tredwell! Now harken closely to what I say. There is an unseen thread that separates life from afterlife, and this thread cannot be broken. I am not empowered to effect any substantive changes in your existence. I can merely guide you toward the answers that shall then be forthcoming. List, now. There is a portmanteau in the attic that will illuminate many things.

I entreat you, seek it out. Once unearthed, the unearthly shall be revealed."

That said, the spirit made a military salute, clicked the heels of his boots together, turned his back to Amy, and was gone, leaving only darkness in the room.

Amy jumped out of bed and flicked on the wall switch. The room was definitely empty and the window was closed.

Suddenly Jamie pushed open the door. "What's wrong in here?" he asked, rubbing his eyes and yawning. "I heard you shouting. Did you have a nightmare?"

"No, a visitor." Amy ran toward her brother and hugged him tightly.

"Say, what's up?" he asked, pushing her away. "Are you going nuts or something?"

"Maybe, but I hope not. I think I've just seen a ghost."

Jamie yawned again. "So it was a nightmare, eh?"

"No, it was real, I swear it. There was this ghost in the room, Jamie. He wore a funny outfit, and he said he was a relative—at least I think he said that. Anyway, he seems to know something about the skeleton at school—only I don't know what and he wouldn't tell me. He said he's not allowed to or something."

Jamie sat down on the bed, still trying to shake the sleep from his brain. "Is this for real, or what? You said you were psychic, but you never told me you see *ghosts*."

"I never have, not before tonight. Well, maybe I have—sort of; but I didn't know it until now. Anyway, he doesn't want to be called a ghost. He says he's a spirit."

"You mean you actually talked to this guy?"

"Yes, that's what I'm telling you. He was wearing some uniform and looked like George Washington."

"You talked to *George Washington*?"

Amy felt like screaming. "No, I didn't say that. He wore a uniform like Washington's, but he said his name was Tredwell."

"You mean you were talking to the ghost of Grandpa Tredwell?"

Amy stamped her feet. "No, Jamie, I don't know who I was talking to!"

The sleep finally began to clear from Jamie's mind. "Okay, calm down. What did this ghost or spirit or whatever say to you?"

"Lots of things I didn't understand. He talks real funny— sort of old-fashioned. Oh, yes, he said something about a man's toe hidden in the attic."

"A *what*?"

"Well— I *think* that's what he said. The toe has something to do with the skeleton at school." Amy could see the skeptical expression on her brother's face. "Oh, Jamie, you do believe me, don't you? It wasn't my imagination, *really*. This spirit was *here*."

Jamie sighed. "Okay, I'm trying to think logically. At first I didn't believe you when you said you were psychic, but that's a fact. And I don't want to believe you now, either, but I guess I'd better. All right, let's assume for the moment that you did see a ghost."

"*Spirit*."

"Whatever. You say he came to tell you something about a man's toe up in the attic?"

"Well," said Amy cautiously, "I'm not certain; I might've gotten that part wrong."

"Let's hope so for our sake," he pleaded, grabbing his sister's arm.

"Where are we going?"

"Up to the attic, naturally. If this guy is so anxious for you to find something, you'd better start looking!"

The pungent aroma of dried flowers and herbs seemed to permeate the attic. The air was so warm and heavy, Amy felt as if someone were breathing down the back of her neck.

Jamie directed the flashlight's beam toward the corner wall. "Can you believe it? Mom still has our old rocking horse stored up here. Doesn't she ever clean this place up?"

"No, you won't find anything on that side," said Amy. "I've a strange feeling we're supposed to look through Grandpa Tredwell's things. Mom said they were all piled up here somewhere."

"Oh really?" asked Jamie dubiously, making his way past the broken brass daybed, wicker baskets, and rusty bicycles. "Do you think Grandpa Tredwell collected men's toes?"

Amy encouraged him on. "You're getting warmer, I can feel it. I think it's somewhere in that pile of boxes."

The twins began opening several cartons, all of which held their late grandfather's books.

"We could be up here all night." Jamie groaned.

Giving up, he cast the flashlight up against the roof's beams, then across the attic walls.

"That's him!" Amy shouted as the light fell against a corner. "That's the *ghost*. He's up here in the attic with us, Jamie!"

Amy could see the tall stately figure proudly standing in his military uniform. His eyes looked stern but kindly, and his white-gloved hand clasped the sword by his side.

"That's no ghost," said Jamie, "it's only a portrait."

"My gosh, you're right, but that's *him*."

"This is the guy who spoke to you tonight?"

"In the flesh— Well, you know."

The twins approached the portrait. Tacked onto the base of the gilded wood frame was a small plaque bearing the name *Jebediah Aloysious Tredwell.*

"Hey, he's some ancestral relative, Amy."

"That's right, that's what he called me. This portrait must've belonged to Grandpa. Oh, you do believe me now, don't you, Jamie?"

"Listen, I'm beginning to believe all sorts of crazy things. Even so, I don't know what this guy wants. And what does he have to do with Hillcrest, the skeleton, and a *man's toe?*" As Jamie flashed the light around the area near the portrait, he noticed a large brocaded bag with leather handles resting against the wall. "Boy, are you a dummy, Amy. We're supposed to be looking for a *portmanteau.*"

"What's that?"

"A *bag*, you idiot. C'mon, let's open it."

The large satchel had the initials *J.A.T.* emblazoned on

the leather. Inside were several private diaries with leather bindings and one much larger book with yellowed manila pages. The portmanteau also contained dozens of drawings and sketches. Underneath each picture were notations written in small precise script, almost impossible to decipher in the semidarkness.

"This looks like a campaign diary," said Jamie. "I guess this fellow Tredwell fought in the Revolution, and this must've been his record of the war."

"That's the clue we're looking for," said Amy. "I feel it in my bones."

"Okay, let's bring it downstairs. Maybe we can ask Mom and Dad about this guy Tredwell in the morning. But right now I've gotta get some *sleep*!"

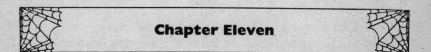

Chapter Eleven

"JEBEDIAH TREDWELL?" ASKED MRS. FERGUSON, POURING HER morning coffee. "Surely I've told you children about him. He's our most famous relative, I *must* have told you."

"No, you never did," said Jamie. "We found lots of his stuff in the attic last night, and we'd like to know who he was."

"He was a lieutenant colonel in Washington's army," explained his mother, buttering some toast. "He saw several battles: Brandywine Creek, the siege of Yorktown. In fact, he was with Washington at Valley Forge."

"Really?" Amy said. "Did he die during that cruel winter when the soldiers had no boots and froze to death?" She didn't like to think that she had been visited by a spirit who had met such an unfortunate and untimely death.

Mrs. Ferguson laughed. "No, he died in his sleep under satin coverlets at the age of eighty-four."

"Eighty-four?" asked Amy. "That's impossible. The man I saw was much younger."

"What did you say, dear?"

"Never mind, Mom; go ahead."

"Well, Jebediah led a very rich, full life. After the war he became a wealthy merchant, traveled throughout the world, then returned here to Monroe to spend his final years."

"Did he live here?" asked Jamie, still trying to determine why the spirit would be haunting the house.

"No, he had a grand estate, but this was part of Jebediah's property. In fact, the spot our house now stands on was originally his apple orchard. A few of his old trees still survive in our yard, but most of them were cut down long ago."

Things were finally beginning to make sense to Amy. Once before, she'd sensed the spirit near the apple trees outside.

Mrs. Ferguson filled a platter with scrambled eggs and placed it on the table. "I can't believe I never told you about Jebediah. When I was little, your grandpa Tredwell told me so many fascinating stories about him, I think I fell a little bit in love with him. His life seemed so brave, daring, and romantic."

"What's that, Miriam?" asked Mr. Ferguson, who was just entering the kitchen. "Exactly *who* are you in love with?"

"Jebediah Tredwell," his wife answered, grinning.

"Aha, bragging about the old family ancestry, eh? Well, kids, there was no one so grand on *my* side of the family. Blacksmiths and butchers, yes, but no personal friends of General Washington."

"Was he really a friend of George Washington?" asked Amy.

"Certainly," said her mother. "In fact, when Washington was elected president, he asked Jebediah Tredwell to join his first cabinet, but he declined."

"Know why?" added Mr. Ferguson teasingly. "I think he had wild oats to sow. He was still a comparatively young man when the war was over. Yes, I suspect Jebediah was quite a fellow in his day—broke many hearts, no doubt, and never married."

Mrs. Ferguson nudged her husband under the kitchen table. "I never should have told you I once had a crush on him."

"Maybe that's why you never told *us* about him," Amy commented. "We didn't even know you had his portrait."

"That belonged to your grandfather," she explained. "It's one of the things I might donate to the Historical Society someday—if I ever get organized. I think there are lots of Jebediah's diaries in the attic too. I often read them when I was little. I remember he wrote that whenever he had a problem, he would stroll through his apple orchard to work it out. Don't think me silly, but when I was about your age, I often sensed he might still be around somewhere."

"You mean a *ghost*?" Amy asked.

"Well, no—it was just a feeling I had sometimes."

"Part of her schoolgirl crush," explained Mr. Ferguson. "But then *I* came along and changed all that."

A faint blush crossed Mrs. Ferguson's cheeks. "That's right, Richard, you did. That's when I forgot all about the dashing Revolutionary War officer and his diaries."

"We found his sketchbook too," Jamie said. "He was a pretty good artist."

"Listen, you're welcome to look through all those things," said his father, "but treat them with respect. We history professors don't like to think of peanut butter being smeared on antique manuscripts. Come to think of it, since you're not going to school until next week, reading through that campaign diary might make a good lesson. As I always say, if you can make history come alive, you can make history fascinating."

Amy was far from being fascinated by history, but she was dying to read the campaign diary. What could it possibly have to do with Boney Mahoney? The connection seemed baffling.

Amy was no longer upset by the strange apparition she'd seen the night before. Knowing Jebediah was a famous relative seemed to make a difference. Somehow, she sensed he was truly trying to solve the mystery she and Jamie found themselves involved in.

That afternoon the twins pored over Jebediah's campaign diary. It contained illlustrations of several of the famous battles of the Revolutionary War and mentioned many loyalists and patriots by name. Jebediah had sketched the troops of militiamen and described their encampments. Tredwell had made many drawings of his comrade in arms and good friend Sergeant Cornelius Garver. Apparently Garver had saved Tredwell's life on more than one occasion.

"This stuff is all very interesting," said Jamie, "but it's not getting us anywhere."

"We have to keep reading," said Amy. "I'm sure there's a clue in here somewhere."

Jamie had reached the part where Tredwell described the army's winter encampment at Valley Forge. "Listen to this," he said: " 'We have now come upon the cruelest of times. We not only have shortages of food and clothing, but many of our men go without shoes. For want of blankets, many are obliged to sit by the fires all night. The general informs me a young nobleman from France, the marquis de Lafayette, will soon be joining us. French aid is imperative at this point.' " On the next page a sad notation followed: " 'My dearest friend and comrade, Cornelius Garver, is missing. Indeed, this is the darkest moment of a bleak, dark winter. His body goes undiscovered, and one must assume the snow shall be his only burial ground. Would that I could create a more fitting final resting place for such a brave, noble, trustworthy companion.' "

Amy took the book from her brother and started leafing through the pages. She glanced at each of the detailed sketches that Tredwell had drawn of his friend Garver. "That's him," she said excitedly, "I'm sure of it. It makes perfect sense because Garver's body was never found or buried. I *know* that's him."

"Who?" asked Jamie.

"Boney Mahoney, of course."

"You mean our school skeleton is actually Sergeant Garver? Well, how on earth did he get from Valley Forge to Hillcrest?"

"I don't know. And I don't know what *I'm* supposed to do about it either."

Jamie shrugged. "Neither do I. I guess you'll have to try contacting Tredwell's ghost again. Only, this time *I'm* going to be around when he appears!"

Late that night the twins stood in Amy's bedroom as she tried concentrating her psychic energy.

"This is *stupid*," she grumbled. "I don't know how to contact a spirit. So far all I have is a headache."

"Try *harder*. You have to make that guy materialize."

Amy shut her eyes tight. "It's no use," she complained, "I've been concentrating like crazy and nothing happens."

Suddenly she heard a strange echoing sound fill the room. Then she opened her eyes and stared into the face of Jebediah Tredwell.

"Why look you in the wrong direction, child? I come not from without but from within. Pray, what is your problem?"

"*My* problem?" she asked. "I thought *you* were the one with the problem, and I can't help solve it unless you *tell* me something."

Jamie stared at his sister. "Amy, why are you talking to the wall?"

Amy stared back. "That isn't a wall, it's Jebediah Tredwell. Don't you *see* him?"

Jamie looked closer. It was definitely a blank wall. "There's nothing there; just a blank."

Indignant, Jebediah put his hand to his hips. "Impudent puppy," he said, scowling. "The light shall shine through your carcass should you call *me* nothing. You must be mad as the winds!"

"Uh-oh," said Amy. "I think you made him angry, Jamie."

Jamie was still staring at emptiness. "Me? What did I say? I can't even *see* him. In fact, I don't believe he's there."

"Hang me for a rogue if I'm not," the lieutenant colonel shouted.

Amy felt her head begin to throb, and she threw herself across the bed. "What a mess," she moaned. "You can't see Jebediah, and I don't know how to help him by myself."

The spirit seemed concerned. "What ails you, child? Look you now, take a cephalic plaster for your headache. Mercy on my life, I've distressed you. Are you distraught because your brother cannot comprehend me?"

"He's the smart one," she explained. "I can't figure things out on my own, and we need information. Why can't Jamie see you?"

"Each of us has different gifts, Cousin. Now then, I shall address your brother more civilly, if that be your wish." The spirit strolled past Amy's bed and approached her brother. "Greetings, Cousin," he said, smiling. Then he patted Jamie on the head.

Jamie still didn't see anything, but he felt a strange

85

sensation on top of his head, as if someone had touched it. "What's that?" he asked.

"It's *him*," Amy explained. "He wants to make friends with you, even though you can't see him."

Jamie felt both awkward and foolish. "Oh yeah? Well, I guess any relative of Amy's is a relative of mine, too, so here goes." He extended his hand toward the empty space in front of him. To his surprise, he felt it being clasped by another in a handshake. "Hey," he said excitedly, "I think we just shook hands."

"That's right," said Amy. "See, I *told* you he was here."

Jamie thought it best to be friendly. "Okay, Tredwell old buddy. I guess you must be around here somewhere, but why can't I see you?"

"My spirit is within your grasp," replied Jebediah, "but you do not invite its appearance as your sister does. Long before she was born, she was predestined to become a link connecting other aspects of life."

Jamie continued staring at what he still perceived to be a blank wall. "Did he answer me?"

"Yes, Jamie. I think he said you might see him someday, but you can't right now."

"*Someday* isn't good enough," he argued. "Oh, this is silly! *You* better ask him the questions, Amy. I'll just sit here and wait for a *translation*." Disgusted, Jamie sat down in the chair by the bed and picked up a magazine. "You guys just go about your business," he said sarcastically, "don't mind me."

"Lieutenant Colonel Tredwell," Amy said politely, "we have some questions."

"Call me Jebediah—or Jeb, should you wish," he said, smiling. "Kindred relations mustn't stand on ceremony."

"Well, *Jeb*, can you answer questions?"

"Only inasmuch as they may give guidance. What do you wish to know?"

"We need to know about Sergeant Garver," she explained.

"To be sure. He was the finest of comrades. His loss still grieves my heart. The man was never panegyrical—not like many of his sort, continually in scrapes and roundhouses. He once saved my life when our troops were ambuscaded."

Amy winced. "This isn't going to work, Jamie," she whispered. "I can't understand a word Jeb is saying."

"Have you no wit, girl?" the colonel shouted. "I tell you, Garver was a soldier and a gentleman. Need I say more?"

"Yes, you do." Amy was insistent. "*Lots* more. You have to tell us if he's the skeleton out at Hillcrest."

Jebediah shook his head sadly. "This much only can I acknowledge. My dear friend's spirit is not at rest. These many years he and I have waited for a soul responsive to his plight. And these many years his bones have sought the ultimate haven of the flesh which has been denied him. Yet you have it within your power to correct this."

"How?"

"Would that I could tell you. I ask your pardon for my vagueness, but it needs must be so. This much I can tell

87

you: If ever a man did good in the world, it was Cornelius Garver. This is why his spirit's present anguish calls me back from the past. And yet *I* am powerless to assist him, for *you* are the avenue of hope. Attend me, child; enlist your brother's aid in this endeavor, and success shall be yours. Together you embody the power of both the mind and the spirit—an efficacious combination."

With that last remark Jebediah disappeared.

"Did he really say that?" asked Jamie after his sister had recounted her entire conversation with Colonel Tredwell. "He thinks we should be a *team*?"

"Sure," said Amy, "and I think Jebediah is right. I may have psychic gifts, but you're the clever one. *I* don't know how to help that poor skeleton at Hillcrest. I feel sorry for him, but what am I supposed to do?"

"*Bury* him, of course," Jamie said matter-of-factly. "I'm sure that's why he's making all this fuss. Look, he was a brave soldier who wants a decent burial, that's all."

"You're right," said Amy. "What a perfectly logical explanation. Sure, all we have to do is bury him. Hey, wait a minute. How can we do that?"

"Simple. Just tell people who the skeleton really is. Someone will probably be glad to give him a funeral."

"We can't tell anyone that—not without revealing what Jebediah told me. And if we do, everyone will know I'm psychic. No, Jamie, we can't tell *anyone*."

"Okay, okay," he replied. "Well, I can see this whole thing's up to me now. *I'm* going to have to figure out some clever way of solving *everything*."

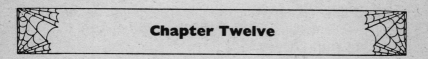

Chapter Twelve

"PLEASE SIT DOWN," SAID MISS APTHORP, ESCORTING THE TWINS into her living room. "I'm so glad you both stopped by. I wanted to speak with you personally before school re-opens next week."

As Amy sat down on the large floral-patterned sofa, she glanced around the room. She'd never been inside Miss Apthorp's house before, but it was just as she'd imagined it: neat, orderly, and a touch old-fashioned with its chintz, doilies, and the lovely chiming clock above the mantel.

"Have some cake, children." Miss Apthorp lifted the silver tray from the tea cart. "Try the petit fours, they're marvelous."

Amy selected a square with pink icing, and Jamie grabbed a chocolate one. Before they had taken a bite,

Miss Apthorp piled several more of the small cakes onto individual china plates, which she then placed on their laps. "Now then," she said, smiling, "what can I do for you both? You know I'm in your debt for the clever way you figured things out at school. Naturally, I plan to have a special assembly in your honor when Hillcrest reopens."

Jamie gulped down his petit four. "No, Miss Apthorp, please don't make a big deal about this back at school. It would make me and Amy feel uncomfortable."

Miss Apthorp looked extremely disappointed; she loved special assemblies. "Oh? Well then, what can I do to show my appreciation?"

"Would you do *anything*?" Amy asked.

"Certainly. Anything within reason, that is."

"We do have one request," Jamie began, "but it might seem sort of odd."

Miss Apthorp laughed gaily. "*Nothing* would seem odd to me after the bizarre events of the past week!"

"Well, we'd like you to *give* us something," Amy said.

"A gift?" she asked. "Yes, I suppose you do deserve some reward. After all, you helped capture a criminal."

"Oh, we don't want *money*," Jamie said. "I know you might think this is crazy, but we'd like you to give us Boney Mahoney."

"Our school skeleton? What on earth for?"

"We need it," said Amy.

"For our project," added Jamie.

"What project?" asked Miss Apthorp.

"We can't tell you," said Jamie, "not yet, anyway. But if the project works out, we can tell you then."

Their headmistress thought a moment. "You're right, this is an odd request. But under the circumstances it's the least I can do. All right, I'll turn over the skeleton to you. As a matter of fact, I was thinking of buying a new one for the biology lab. They have some marvelous plastic versions on the market nowadays. Not that I'm superstitious, mind you, but some of the younger children may have unpleasant memories in that regard. I'm also planning to have Alexander Cartwright's portrait restored, so that Hillcrest will really be back to normal shortly."

"That's swell," said Jamie. "Can we pick him up right away?"

"Pick *who* up?" Miss Apthorp asked.

"Boney Mahoney."

"Oh— Well, yes, I suppose so. I still have a guard stationed on the property. I'll notify him to let you in. Goodness, I had no idea you children were so interested in osteology!"

"I'm not sure I've got this message right," said the security guard. "Did Miss Apthorp say you kids were here to pick up a *skeleton*?"

"That's right," said Jamie, "she gave us permission."

"Sorry. Don't know where to find a skeleton. Can you kids find it yourselves?"

"Sure," said Amy. "It's down in the basement. We'll let ourselves in."

Jamie felt himself tense as they walked around the side entrance toward the basement door. "I'm nervous," he admitted. "You think Boney Mahoney is still lying behind the door? What if he tries to attack us again?"

Amy stood motionless, staring at the closed door for a moment. "He won't," she said. "He knows we're here to help him and that we're relatives of Jebediah."

"Really? How does he know that?"

Shutting her eyes, she placed the palms of her hands on the door. "Because I'm sending him a psychic message. Wait . . . I think I'm also getting some kind of message back."

"From Boney Mahoney?"

"From Cornelius Garver. He wants to tell us that his spirit animates the skeleton but it's actually only bones that can't harm anyone."

"Ask him if we can take the bones away."

"Yes. Garver's spirit is detached from the skeleton now, so we can take it—as long as we don't hurt it."

"Tell him we promise to take good care of it," said Jamie.

Amy continued directing her thoughts toward the skeleton on the opposite side of the door, and she responded intuitively to the answers coming from its owner. "I think he wants to know *where* we're taking him, Jamie."

"Tell him we're going to pay a visit to a famous professor at Monroe University. Someone who can bring him to life again!"

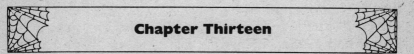

Chapter Thirteen

THE TWINS FELT EXTREMELY PECULIAR. THEY REALIZED THAT TWO large denim bags were hardly proper wrapping for a hero of the Revolution, but it was all they could find in the basement—and it was certainly better than having to drag the skeleton through town naked.

It wouldn't be proper, Amy thought, to take him on the bus, and they had no money for a taxi, so they decided to walk all the way from Hillcrest to the campus of Monroe. Jamie walked in front supporting half the skeleton on his shoulder, and Amy walked behind with the lighter half on her shoulder.

They didn't want to attract attention but found it was impossible not to. Heidi Wentworth was the first to notice them, on Elmhurst Drive. "What's in the bag?" she asked.

"None of your business," said Jamie.

On Spencer Street, Emile Bruckner was coming out of the Pantry Spoon luncheonette as they approached. "Hey, kids, did you see you made the front page the other day? You two did some great police work."

They nodded but didn't stop.

"What's in those laundry bags?" asked Mr. Bruckner.

"Nothing special," said Jamie, readjusting the weight on his shoulder. As he did, the skeleton's arm slipped through an opening in the bag.

"Oh?" Mr. Bruckner said suspiciously. The man definitely had a nose for news. "Looks to me like a bag of bones. What are you kids up to—and is there a good story in it?"

Amy slipped the arm back inside the laundry bag, then smiled discreetly. "If there is, you'll be the first to know."

It seemed like ages before they finally arrived at the campus of Monroe University. Everyone there knew the Ferguson twins personally: the security guards, faculty, and staff. Once each week, from the time they were babies, Mr. Ferguson would take his children with him to work. From the age of six, they'd been allowed to sit in on their father's history classes. Mr. Ferguson referred to this as "education by osmosis"—a method that had worked wonderfully with Jamie but had never been of much academic benefit to his sister. Amy had always preferred to spend the time running through the corridors and peeking in at classroom windows at random.

But today the twins had a definite destination as they hurried up the steps of the Frommer Science Building. "I hope the professor will be in his office," said Jamie. "We can't carry these bones around all day."

They took the elevator to the second floor, then knocked on the door that said Professor Schiller, Paleontology.

Professor Schiller was one of Amy's favorite people at Monroe University. When she was younger, he had come to visit every Sunday. Before dinner Professor Schiller would help the twins construct marvelous clay sculptures of prehistoric animals and tell the stories of their origins. The study of fossils was his area of interest professionally, but modeling the outward appearance of living creatures from their bones was a compelling hobby that had turned into a kind of second profession. Professor Schiller liked to call it "reconstructive detective work," and the twins had always been fascinated by it.

Once, Jamie had found the skeleton of a small animal behind the house, but he and Amy couldn't agree on whether it was a field mouse, a squirrel, or a chipmunk. To solve the argument, Professor Schiller reconstructed its body in clay; it was, they discovered, actually a small jackrabbit, which they then gave a proper burial underneath a lilac tree.

Their father always said, "If you have a question regarding bones, Sam Schiller is your man." And the twins definitely had a big question, which they hoped the professor could help them solve quickly.

"Come in," called out a voice from behind the door.

As always, it was difficult to find Professor Schiller, the one *living* specimen in an office filled with plastic and clay replicas of Neanderthal man, Cro-Magnon man, Java man, Rhodesian man. But today, as usual, he sat at his polished mahogany desk, behind an ordered stack of leather-bound books and medical manuscripts.

The professor's fluffy tufts of white hair and round rosy cheeks had always reminded Amy of Santa Claus. "Ah, my two favorite students," he greeted them, smiling. "What on earth have you brought me?"

"It's a skeleton," said Jamie as he unwrapped it.

"Well, so it is," said the professor. "Seat him in the easy chair, Jamie, where he can be comfortable."

Professor Schiller had a reverence for bones some might consider eccentric. To his mind, every bone had not only a story but a history, and an entire skeleton was always to be treated with extreme respect.

Pushing his spectacles down on his nose, he circled the chair several times, carefully observing the skeleton. "I rarely receive so handsome a visitor. Yes, he's quite a fine-looking gentleman."

Amy was impressed. "You already know it's a man?"

"Oh, without a doubt. You see, the female skull is usually smaller than the male and also lighter. The forehead of a woman's skull is usually less sloping than this one, the supraorbital region is less developed, and the mastoid smaller also."

"Can you tell how old he was?" asked Jamie.

Studiously the professor examined the skeleton further. "This is a bit more difficult. The biological age of an individual rarely coincides with the calendrical age. Under fifty-five, for certain. This gentleman's skull sutures are not yet obliterated. The teeth are good too. His dental arch hadn't yet become flat. Judging from the shape of his lower jaw, I'd say he was definitely under forty, perhaps even thirty, but I'd have to do some tests to verify that." Sliding his spectacles back up, Professor Schiller looked at the children quizzically. "Would it be presumptuous of me to ask where you *found* this gentleman?"

"He's been in the biology lab at Hillcrest for years," Jamie explained. "Amy and I think we might know who he is—or was. Could you make a clay reconstruction of his head for us?"

"You wish a facial reconstruction?"

"Yes," said Amy, "it's very important."

"Well, a facial reconstruction from this skull would be a laborious process. First, I must reproduce the masticatory and neck muscles, then comes the modeling of the facial mask. The nasal bones must be determined, and the configuration of the glabella, as well as the outer form of the alveolar region of the upper jaw. Then comes the mouth, which is also tricky. I must calibrate the width of the dental arc. For the eyes, I'll need to take into account the shape of the margins of the orbits, the degree and projection of the eyeball. For the ear, I must observe the construction of the temporal bones, not to mention the direction, size, and shape of the auditory meatus. Then—"

"Please, Professor," interrupted Jamie, "it's really *terribly* important."

The professor pondered the proposal. "Ah, for my two little fossils, I would do *anything*. When do you wish this done?"

"As soon as possible?" Amy pleaded.

"That soon, eh? Well, this *must* be important. All right, consider it done. I will go into my laboratory right now and work all evening if necessary. Perhaps you'd care to join me there?"

Carefully Professor Schiller lifted the skeleton into his arms. "Don't worry, young man, you're in good hands."

The twins followed the professor down the hall and into the elevator, which they took to his laboratory on the fourth floor. Professor Schiller's lab looked more like an artist's studio. There were clay busts and plaster molds scattered about, some finished, some still in the process of construction. Amy noticed a clay model of a young woman's head on a pedestal and somehow knew immediately that something awful had happened to her.

As the professor laid the skeleton on the table, he noticed Amy staring at the model. "Ah, such a sad story," he said. "Last year the New York Police Department sent me this young woman's remains. Her skull had been unearthed at a building site in Manhattan."

"Did something terrible happen to her?" asked Amy.

"Yes, poor thing. Her name was Maria Petrov. Her family had declared her missing more than thirty years earlier. Murder, I'm afraid, and the murderer is still unknown."

"Who's this one?" asked Jamie, pointing to a clay bust of a sinister-looking man with harshly cruel features.

"Ah, that was my first major reconstruction. It's Ivan the Terrible, the czar of Russian in the sixteenth century. His sarcophagus was opened many years ago. The Russian Ministry of Culture called me in to work on that case. My model agrees entirely with descriptions by his contemporaries. A most successful venture."

Jamie was impressed. "No kidding? Well, he certainly was nasty-looking."

"I must prepare the plasticene now," explained the professor. "Very shortly your mysterious gentleman will also have a face."

Jamie could hear his stomach rumbling. "I'm *starving*. Can't we go out for burgers or something?"

"We'd better wait until the professor is finished," said Amy, trying to calm her own hunger.

"What'd Mom say when you called home?"

"I told her we're at the university, and she said to be home by nine."

"I hope Professor Schiller is finished by then."

Watching the professor work was like observing a fine artist in the heat of creation. Slowly and carefully he made calibrations and calculations, then began modeling clay onto the skull of the skeleton. At first it just looked like lumpy blobs, but as the professor continued, definite features began to emerge. The eye sockets took on a distinct expression. Gradually the teeth were covered over to form the shape of a small, finely contoured mouth, and the skeletal jawbone soon became a strong, determined chin. Within a matter of hours the skeleton had taken on a new personality. He now bore the face of a kind and friendly person.

Professor Schiller stood back to admire this own handiwork. "It seems this fellow was quite a good-looking young man. Well, children, my task is done. Have I helped you to determine exactly who he is?"

"Oh, yes," said Amy admiringly. "You did a *wonderful* job. It looks exactly like him!"

"We have some drawings in an old sketchbook," explained Jamie, "and your reconstruction matches them perfectly."

Professor Schiller seemed pleased his work had been so successful. "In that case, I believe a formal introduction is appropriate."

"Sure," said Amy. "Professor, let me introduce you to Sergeant Cornelius Garver. He was a soldier in the American Revolution who fought very bravely for his country. I'm afraid he froze to death at Valley Forge."

"Ah, a *patriot*." The professor nodded and then bowed toward the skeleton. "A distinct honor, sir," he said, and shook the bony hand. "In my small way, I feel I put flesh on the bare bones of history, but people such as yourself are the ones who *made* it. In your case, my detective work has been extremely rewarding." Laying the skeleton down on the table, he placed a sheet across it. "Now, children, perhaps we three might celebrate with some *food*? I'm ravenous and the cafeteria down-stairs is still open."

Jamie bit into his burger with pleasure. "Could you do just a little more detective work for us, Professor? Your reconstruction proves the skeleton is who we thought he was, but we still don't know how he got from where he was to where we found him."

Professor Schiller blew on his chicken soup. "Such curiosity you children have!" he said admiringly. "It's hard for me to believe I'm sitting here with Miriam and Richard's little fossils, discussing aspects of forensic science and paleontology. Why, I can remember when I changed your diapers!"

Amy blushed. "It's really important we figure this all out, Professor."

The professor feigned a scowl. "No, Amy, I do no more until you call me what you used to when you were still a little acorn."

Amy thought back to the many happy times in the past when the professor had crawled around the floor after her, playing catch. Delighted, Amy would scream, then crawl away. "Do you mean *Fessy*?" she asked.

"That's it," he said with delight. "*Fessy*. Ah, it makes me feel *young* again!" After throwing a generous amount of crackers into his soup, he quickly gobbled it down. "Now, what more do you children need to know?"

"Well," said Jamie, "we now have *proof* the skeleton is actually Sergeant Garver who died over two hundred years ago. But Garver died at Valley Forge, hundreds of miles away from here. We can't figure out how he wound up in Monroe County. As far as I know, he's been in the biology lab at Hillcrest since the school opened fifty years ago."

The professor nodded. "A most intriguing puzzle, but one not without precedent. Shall I tell you an interesting story? This one involves a skull, not an entire skeleton, but it illustrates the point. There was once a famous English Shakespearean actor named George Frederick Cooke, who died in New York City in 1812. Sadly, he was a drunkard and a pauper at the time. His doctor, in lieu of payment, got permission to sever Cooke's head before the body was buried."

"How awful," said Amy, "why'd he do *that*?"

"Because Cooke was considered a creative genius, Amy. The doctor wished to make some phrenological investigations of his skull—which he did, along with several of his friends, one of them being Daniel Webster."

"No kidding," said Jamie.

"Indeed. At the time this was considered legitimate scientific study. But as the years passed, Cooke's skull seems to have popped up in the strangest places. Legend has it Edwin Booth once used it in his production of *Hamlet*. He also made a tiepin from one of Cooke's teeth. That tooth is now in a museum, and the remainder of the skull resides at Jefferson Medical College in Philadelphia."

"A fascinating story," said Jamie, "Disgusting, but fascinating. Only, I don't see what it has to do with *our* skeleton."

"Both grave robbing and body snatching were lucrative

occupations in the eighteenth century," explained the professor. "Medical students were willing to pay handsomely for anatomical samples. It may seem ghoulish, but this is how medical surgery has progressed. Very possibly Sergeant Garver has resided in various locations. Then again, perhaps only his skeletal remains were sold long after his death."

"Oh, I get it," said Jamie, remembering the assortment of oddities belonging to Alexander Cartwright that were still stored in Hillcrest's basement. "Cartwright collected some pretty weird things. He might've picked up the skeleton in his travels."

"More than likely," the professor agreed. "Mr. Cartwright would have no way of knowing the skeleton's history. Skull reconstruction is a comparatively new field of investigation."

"Which *you* originated, right?" asked Amy.

"Well, yes, I was one of the first in the field," the professor said proudly. "But there is still much to learn. So you see, it's not unusual for a fine skeletal specimen to pass through several hands during many lifetimes. You proved that point yourself today."

"How do you mean?" asked Jamie.

"Well, just yesterday your skeleton was at Hillcrest, and tonight it is in my laboratory."

"Poor Sergeant Garver." Amy sighed. "He's been waiting such a long time for a decent burial. It's our job to make sure he gets one."

Professor Schiller nodded knowingly. "Ah, so this is your important project. You children wish to terminate this page of history: an admirable intention. Naturally, the young gentleman is welcome to stay in my lab, but a burial ceremony would undoubtedly be more appropriate."

"That's it," said Jamie excitedly. "A *ceremony*. Gee thanks, Professor, you've been a tremendous help. And you've given me a fantastic idea!"

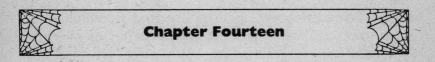

Chapter Fourteen

"I GIVE UP!" SAID MRS. FERGUSON, STRUGGLING THROUGH THE morning mail. "I have this tremendous task and not a soul to help me with it!"

The twins and their father were preparing Saturday brunch—a ritual in the Ferguson household. No one was allowed to leave the house until they'd consumed at least two courses. During brunch the family always sat down together to discuss the week's problems, giving priority to the most important. Richard Ferguson called this family rap session "food for thought." It was also a time to experiment with various ingenious ways of making breakfast.

This particular morning Mr. Ferguson had thrown bean sprouts in with the eggs, and Jamie had added apple sauce to the pancakes. Amy didn't care for either.

"Sounds like your mother has the priority situation today," said Mr. Ferguson. "Sit down, Miriam, and we'll talk it out. What's in the mail that bothers you so much?"

"Idiot answers, that's what," she said, tasting the omelet. "Richard, what on earth did you put in this?"

"Sprouts. Don't you like them?"

"Not particularly. Sprouts are for salads, not eggs."

"If you don't like the eggs," said Amy, "don't try the pancakes. They taste like sweet sponges."

Mr. Ferguson frowned. "You liberated women should reeducate your taste buds—or else prepare yourselves to return to the kitchen. In case you haven't noticed, Jamie and I are deeply involved in culinary creativity."

"I thought we were discussing *my* problem, Richard."

"I'm all ears; fire away."

"Well, I sent out questionnaires to all the members of the Historical Society asking what they thought might be a good benefit fund-raiser."

"And?"

"And most of them came up with the most ridiculous proposals. The Harrisons said they'd like to have a flower show, but it's autumn, so that's impossible. The Whitneys suggested we put on a musical."

"That sounds all right."

"Maybe. But it's actually just an excuse for Harold to sing 'The Impossible Dream.' Harold sings that song at every party we've been to, and I certainly wouldn't *pay* to hear it!"

"No good suggestions, eh?"

"Not one, Richard. Cynthia Sykes suggested a costume party, but *you* don't like that idea."

"Okay, okay. I'll wear tights if I'm forced into them."

Jamie finished his pancakes (which he found delicious), then sat back, smiling smugly. "Relax, Mom, your problem is solved."

"No, it isn't," she said sharply. "Personally, I don't think a costume party is appropriate. Everyone will probably come as Cleopatra or Napoleon, and—"

"No, Mom, that's not what Jamie means," Amy interrupted. "We sat up all night talking about this, and we've got an idea. We think you should have a truly historical ceremony."

"A ceremony?" she asked. "Commemorating what?"

"The installation of a grave," said Jamie.

"A grave? Whose grave?"

Jamie explained. "We thought it could be something like the Tomb of the Unknown Soldier at Arlington National Cemetery. People come from all over the country to visit that, don't they?"

"That's right," his mother said. "We took you children there last spring."

"Well," Jamie continued, "if lots of people come to visit the grave of an *unknown* soldier, I figure they wouldn't mind paying money to visit the grave of a *known* soldier—especially if he had been a Revolutionary War hero."

"And a close friend of Jebediah Tredwell," Amy added. "That would make it a very special grave, don't you agree?"

Mrs. Ferguson had no idea what her children were driving at. "Yes, I suppose it would, but so what?"

Mr. Ferguson stared at his children. "I think our two

107

little amateur historians must've unearthed something in those diaries."

"That's right, Dad," said Amy. "Jebediah made lots of sketches of his friend Sergeant Garver, who was missing in action and never buried."

"And it just so happens," added Jamie, "that the skeleton in the school lab is actually Cornelius Garver. Professor Schiller proved that to us last night."

Mr. Ferguson nodded. "So that's what you two were doing out so late last night? Making poor Fessy burn the midnight oil?"

"That's right," Jamie admitted. "He reconstructed the skeleton's face for us, and it's definitely Sergeant Garver."

Mrs. Ferguson seemed suspicious. "Wait one minute. Boney Mahoney has been out at Hillcrest for as long as I can remember. How could you children possibly discover his true identity?"

"Well, you see," Jamie began, "Amy has this—"

Kicking her brother under the table, Amy gave him an icy stare. "It was *intuition*, Mom," she explained. "I don't know where the idea came from. Call it a hunch, but it turned out to be right."

"A hunch?" asked her mother. "I suppose that's possible. But why do I feel you're *hiding* something?"

Amy tried looking innocent. No matter what, she was determined to keep her psychic power a secret. "I don't know, Mom. I guess you must be a suspicious person."

"Well, *I'm* not," said Mr. Ferguson. "If this is true, it's the basis for a wonderful historical ceremony. Miriam,

108

it's just the thing you've been looking for to attract attention to the society."

"I guess you're right," Mrs. Ferguson agreed. "A memorial service would attract lots of attention. There's a lovely little piece of land behind the Historical Society which members had planned to turn into a garden. It would make a very nice burial site."

"You could erect a stone and everything," Jamie suggested.

Mrs. Ferguson was becoming increasingly excited by the idea. "That's right. Perhaps Mr. Santucci, the stone-cutter, might donate his services. I wonder what Sergeant Garver might like written on his headstone."

"Amy could ask him," Jamie said automatically, and once again his sister kicked him underneath the table. "I mean—well—maybe we could all ask ourselves what we would like written. Anyway, what do you think of the whole idea?"

"I think it's inspired," said Mr. Ferguson. "I don't know by what, but it's definitely an inspiration."

Mrs. Ferguson agreed. "I'll speak to the society members about it immediately."

Chapter Fifteen

IT WAS A PLAIN OAK COFFIN. JACOB NORSTRUM AT THE LUMBER-yard had spent several days polishing the wood to a lustrous sheen.

For two weeks everyone in Monroe had been involved in the upcoming ceremony. Astrid Ogilvy, the florist, planned to create several lovely wreaths of red, white, and blue carnations. Rabbi Cohen, the Reverend Dr. Morton, and Father Donnelly all prepared touching eulogies to be read aloud at the gravesite. Pâtisserie Dumont offered to bake dozens of cakes and pastries for the tea party to follow the ceremony.

At Hillcrest Miss Apthorp instituted Patriot Week. Students spent each morning studying various aspects of the Revolutionary War. They learned about many famous historical figures. But more important, they learned little-

110

known facts about *ordinary* people—young and old, black and white—who had helped to establish new freedoms in a new land.

Discovering the true identity of a skeleton, which had jokingly been referred to as Boney Mahoney for so many years, had somehow cemented many relationships within the community of Monroe. It also made the local people just a little prouder to be Americans.

The twins felt proud too. After all, their efforts had made the whole event possible. And yet Amy also felt a certain sadness. Everyone in town was looking forward to the following Sunday, when the ceremony would take place on the grounds of the Historical Society. But Mr. Santucci, the stonecutter, still had no inspiration for the gravestone he was donating. Local residents had suggested many possible epitaphs, but none of them seemed quite right.

On Friday afternoon a lingering mist hung in the air following the previous night's rain. Amy set out for a long walk without knowing her destination and found herself at the Monroe cemetery. She strolled among gravestones glistening with dew, until she stumbled upon the grave that she suddenly realized was the one she'd wanted to see.

The message written on it was quite simple:

Here lies Jebediah Aloysious Tredwell
    A soldier
    A gentleman
    A friend
What more was there to say?

Mr. Santucci nodded. "That's nice, Amy. Very simple, but very nice. I'll start carving it on the gravestone right away."

Amy watched as he placed his hammer and chisel on the cool white marble. The headstone was beautiful. It reminded her of a snowdrift—a pile of snow perhaps like those at Valley Forge that fateful winter of 1777–1778.

Mr. Santucci chipped away at the stone, until Amy could see the delicate shape of letters beginning to emerge from the marble. "Could you add one more thing?" she asked. "Put a forget-me-not above his name, okay?"

Mr. Santucci smiled. "Very nice," he repeated.

Sunday was appropriately named; for the sun was a major part of the day. It rose in the east like a red flame and quickly spread its rays across Monroe County. The crisp autumn chill in the air only heightened the sense of expectation surrounding the upcoming proceedings. Chimes in the bell towers of all the Monroe churches rang out in unison, reminding the community of the special event.

As Amy was getting dressed her brother knocked on her door. "Have you spoken to him yet?" he asked.

"Who?"

"What do you mean, *who*? Jebediah, naturally. You know, I've been thinking I might call him Jeb—or maybe JT. Anyway, have you seen him?"

"No," said Amy, brushing her hair. "I guess maybe he won't come again."

112

Jamie was annoyed. "Well, that's gratitude. Because of our efforts, Jeb's old friend is getting a bang-up burial. Practically everyone in town will be at the Historical Society today. Jeb could at least come back to say *thanks*. Is that all ghosts are good for—to *scare* people into getting their way?"

"He's not a ghost," she said defensively. "He's a *spirit*."

"So you told me, but I don't understand the distinction."

Over the past two weeks the twins had received ample praise for having solved the mystery at Hillcrest *and* having unearthed the true identity of the laboratory skeleton. But Jamie still felt a formal thank-you from his dead ancestor would be appropriate.

Amy, too, had hoped to see Jebediah again, but not to have him express his gratitude. She had acquired a strange fondness for the spirit she had only encountered twice. Having read his diaries, she considered him an old friend.

Well, maybe Jamie was right, she thought. Jebediah had gotten what he'd come for, then had gone away. If that was the case, she would miss him. But she wouldn't let it spoil the day's special celebration. "You can't wear *jeans*," she said, noticing her brother's outfit. "We're going to a *funeral*. Go change your clothes and dress more formally."

Jamie stood in the doorway, shaking his head. "You know, Amy, sometimes I'm not sure whether you're psychic or *psycho!*"

It wasn't at all a somber ceremony. Instead, it was both respectful and joyful. A burial plot had been excavated behind the Historical Society building, beside a venerable old chestnut tree.

As Sergeant Garver's oak coffin was slowly lowered into the ground, the twins were given the honor of laying the wreath of carnations on top. The three eulogies were read aloud, then Mr. Santucci unveiled the white marble headstone, which would soon be erected.

Everyone seemed pleased with the inscription:

Here lies Sergeant Cornelius Garver
A soldier
A gentleman
A friend

A cool breeze wafted through the trees, and the sun beamed down on the glistening marble slab. Amy felt a sweet sense of oneness with the moment. She found herself thinking back to something Jebediah had told her: that all time is now. In her mind she was not certain what that meant, yet her heart seemed to understand it. After all this time Sergeant Garver was finally receiving the burial ceremony he so rightly deserved. Somehow, it didn't matter that it had taken more than two hundred years for it to happen. She felt a tingling down the back of her spine, almost as if someone were standing beside her, sharing the joy of the moment.

In his own way Jamie was receiving a revelation as well. He felt closer to his sister than he ever had in the past. For in a strange way the past is what had drawn them together: the same past that had drawn all the townspeople of Monroe into sharing this historic ceremony. He glanced at the reverent faces of the crowd

114

surrounding the gravesite and knew they were all partici-
pating in something special.

At the conclusion of the ceremony members of the
Monroe Choral Society sang "America the Beautiful." They
then requested that everyone join in for the last chorus.

As the white clouds raced across the afternoon sky,
hundreds of voices rose up for the final words:

"And crown thy good with brotherhood
From sea to shining sea!"

"Try the napoleons," Mr. Ferguson was saying. "You
don't have to be a history professor to know they're
delicious."

Anne Shuttlesworth, treasurer of the Historical Society,
glanced around the room excitedly. "This tea party is
going marvelously. We've already received dozens of con-
tributions and promises of dozens more. This is definitely
a historic day for Monroe. The society has never been
blessed with so much attention before."

Nodding, the Reverend Dr. Morton bit into his crois-
sant. "All thanks to your children, Richard. I'd say they
did some pretty sophisticated detective work."

"My wife and I agree. Though we're still not certain
how Amy and Jamie managed all this. Quite frankly, it's
still a mystery to us. You see, Dr. Morton, normally our
kids don't get along too well. So for them to join forces
on a project like this is somewhat of a *miracle*."

Dr. Morton smiled. "In my profession you get accus-
tomed to mysteries—*and* miracles."

"Perhaps they're growing up," Miss Shuttlesworth observed.

Miriam Ferguson was standing behind the dessert table, pouring tea for the guests. Was that the answer? she wondered. Were her children finally growing up and learning to respect each other? Somehow, she sensed there was more to it than that. In the past weeks a new, unfamiliar closeness had developed between the twins— not to mention an element of *secrecy*, which had never existed before either.

"You may be right, Dr. Morton," she said, pouring the minister more tea. "Perhaps we *all* have to live with mysteries."

Chapter Sixteen

Everything had been so special, Amy didn't want the day to end. Darkness had fallen hours earlier, yet she did not move from her perch on the porch steps, and sat staring out toward the apple trees. She longed to hang on to the final traces of an extraordinary day, to postpone the onset of the ordinary day that would follow.

She felt a sudden loneliness. Then she noticed a faint filmy light hovering underneath an apple tree. She jumped up and hurried down the steps. "Jebediah?" she whispered. "Is that you?"

As she drew closer the shape took on the now-familiar appearance of a figure. "I was hoping you'd come back," she said, smiling.

"I have never left," he said softly.

"Were you at the ceremony today?" she asked. "I thought I sensed you there, but I wasn't sure."

"Yes, child. I was the first to arrive and the last to depart." He turned his back to her. "It was a most touching occasion," he added.

Amy thought she heard a slight sniffle. "Jebediah, are you *crying*?"

"Impudent rascal!" he snapped. "There's not one syllable of truth in that remark. Must I remind you once again that I am an *officer*. Tears would be most unseemly. Granted, I was greatly moved, but you must remember to keep a civil tongue in your head when addressing me in future."

"You *were* crying," she said delightedly.

"Don't be insolent," he said sharply. "I'm a *spirit*, above such earthly emotions."

Jebediah was crying; Amy knew that—but she let him have his way. "You're right, I'm sorry. Anyway, I'm glad you came back. I missed you."

"And I you, child. You and your brother have done me an eternal service. Because of your efforts, my dear friend is laid to rest at last. Mark me while this I avow: I am everlastingly in your debt and therefore in your power. Should you ever request my presence for any reason, I should be bound to obey." The gauzy film of light surrounding Jebediah's apparition gradually began to fade. "Yes, mark me well, Cousin," he stated as his voice also began to fade, "we are not done with each other. The eternal thread connecting all things, great and small, slackens at times but then pulls taut again."

118

Amy was confused. "What does that mean?" she asked. "Are you saying I'll see you again?"

Suddenly the glow that had lit up the darkness broke into tiny particles, then began to disappear. The night hung heavily in the sky. Amy stood on the lawn, sniffing the tart scent of apples hanging from the few trees remaining from what was once Jebediah Tredwell's beloved apple orchard.

She could hear her brother shouting from the kitchen window. "Hey, Amy, we just got a telephone call from Emile Bruckner. You and I are going to be front-page news again tomorrow! What do you think of that?"

Amy was silent. She was watching the last particles of light drift off into the distance, as if to become one with the night—and the stars.

"Amy, are you out there, or what?"

"Yes, I'm here."

"Well, don't you think it's terrific?" he asked. "Everyone in Monroe thinks we're great. If this keeps up, we'll be able to start a *scrapbook*. I'm going to pick up at least a dozen copies of the *Gazette* in the morning."

Amy took a deep breath, stared up at the stars for another moment, then went inside.

Mrs. Ferguson had prepared hot chocolate for everyone. "C'mon, kids, this'll hit the spot before you go to bed."

"Remember," said Mr. Ferguson, "despite this momentary fame, it's back to school as usual for you children in the morning."

119

"I guess you're right." Jamie sighed. "It will be back to the ordinary tomorrow."

Amy sipped her hot chocolate in silence.

Somehow, she suddenly knew that for herself and Jamie, *nothing* would ever be ordinary again!